SOLDIER PRINCE'S
SECRET BABY
GIFT

SOLDIER PRINCE'S SECRET BABY GIFT

KATE HARDY

MILLS & BOON

First published in Great Britain 2019
by Mills & Boon, an imprint of HarperCollins*Publishers*
1 London Bridge Street, London, SE1 9GF

Large Print edition 2020

© 2019 Harlequin Books S.A.

Special thanks and acknowledgement are given
to Kate Hardy for her contribution to the
A Crown by Christmas series.

ISBN: 978-0-263-08429-0

MIX
Paper from
responsible sources
FSC **FSC˚ C007454**

This book is produced from independently certified
FSC™ paper to ensure responsible forest management. For
more information visit www.harpercollins.co.uk/green.

Printed and bound in Great Britain
by CPI Group (UK) Ltd, Croydon, CR0 4YY

For Cara Colter and Nina Milne—
it was such fun working with you!

PROLOGUE

May

TEN MINUTES UNTIL MIDNIGHT.

Ten minutes until the charity gala was over and the guests were due to leave, and then another three-quarters of an hour to finish clearing up.

And then Tia could go home to bed.

She was exhausted. She'd already done her usual full shift at the café that day, and Saturdays were always a rushed-off-your-feet day. When she'd got home, all she'd wanted to do was to have a long bath and then curl up on the sofa with her mum to watch a movie. But her old school friend Sadie was managing a charity gala tonight and Tia had promised that she'd help out, serving canapés and clearing glasses, and Tia never went back on her promises. Particularly as the cause—supporting children who'd been bereaved—was so close to her heart; she knew first-hand how it felt to lose a member of your family in the armed forces.

Twice.

Their neighbour, Becky, was keeping an eye out for her mum—as she always did on the few occasions that Grace Phillips managed to persuade her daughter to go out somewhere. In less than an hour, Tia could go home. And tomorrow was late opening, being Sunday, so her shift didn't start until ten. It wasn't so bad. She'd had tougher days.

Though she couldn't shake the feeling that someone was staring at her.

She turned round and caught the eye of a tall, dark-haired man across the room.

There was something very familiar about him. Then again, half the people at the charity gala were household names: everyone from musicians to movie stars to models. All the men were wearing tuxedos, and all the women were wearing the kind of posh frocks and designer shoes Tia would never have been able to afford in a million years. This was another world, one where she was supposed to be invisible—the anonymous waitress who smiled as she served canapés and cleared glasses quickly and efficiently. The guy across the room shouldn't even be noticing her.

As she went out onto the hotel balcony to collect glasses from the abandoned tables, still thinking about him, she realised who he was.

Antonio Valenti.

Prince Antonio of Casavalle, to be precise.

The man who had been her older brother Nathan's best friend, who'd served with him as his team commander in an alliance of international armed forces.

The man who'd broken her heart, and her mum's, four months ago, when he'd brought the news that Nathan had been killed in action. Antonio had delivered the news coldly and calmly: a stoic man in a military uniform who didn't even blink as he told them that Nathan's vehicle had hit a land mine on his last mission and he'd been killed instantly. Tia had been too shocked to say anything, but her mother had collapsed at the news that she'd lost her son the same way as she'd lost her husband, so Tia had had to damp down her own grief to support her mother.

Prince Antonio had clearly cared so little about Nathan that he hadn't even stuck around to comfort Grace Phillips or check that she was all right. He'd left almost as soon as he'd delivered the news. He hadn't even stayed for a cup of tea, let alone turned up at the funeral; and, apart from a formal embossed condolence card which he'd scrawled his name across, he hadn't been in contact with them since.

OK, sure, the man was a prince and he had important official duties as well as being in the army. Tia wasn't stupid. She understood that. But would it have hurt him to spend a few minutes with Grace after delivering the news, just to share some memories of her beloved son with her? Or show his face at Nathan's funeral? Or later, perhaps, he could've sent Grace a photograph or a private note via the Palace press office. It wasn't as if her mother was going to rush to the media and try to get money for it, or sell it online. All Grace had needed was a little gesture to let her know that Nathan had *mattered*.

But there had been nothing from Prince Antonio but silence.

Prince Charming? More like Prince Cold and Uncaring, Tia thought, curling her lip. How on earth had her brother been close friends with someone who was so cold and starchy?

And he was probably only here at the gala because he was attending in an official capacity; a man like him certainly wasn't warm enough to care about the work of the charity, or about the children who'd lost their parents or siblings in war. He certainly wouldn't be there rattling a collecting bucket along with the rest of the volunteer fundraisers or schmoozing people into buying tombola tickets.

She put him resolutely out of her mind and continued stacking glasses on a tray ready to carry through to the kitchens.

Tia Phillips looked absolutely exhausted.

Guilt balled in a hard lump in Antonio's throat.

He'd been there when his second-in-command's vehicle, the one in the convoy in front of his, had been blown up by a land mine. Mercifully, death had been instant, so he knew Nathan hadn't suffered; but Antonio had been shattered by the loss. During his years in the army, his team had become like a family to him. Nathan had been his best friend as well as his second-in-command.

But Antonio had been brought up not to show any emotion in public; as a prince of Casavalle, he was expected to be cool and calm in every situation. He and his elder brother Luca had been brought up knowing their duty always came first. And you never, ever said or did anything that made you look as if you'd lost control of your emotions. That had been reinforced by his military training, so Antonio knew he'd been calm and reserved when he broke the news to Nathan's family.

Too calm and reserved, perhaps, in their eyes.

Antonio knew how much Nathan had loved his family. He knew that Grace Phillips was poorly and that Nathan and his little sister Tia had spent their childhood as her carers rather than having the freedom to be children; and he'd promised Nathan silently by the side of his coffin that he'd keep an eye on Grace and Tia.

But he'd been called away almost immediately on another mission, so he hadn't even been able to attend Nathan's memorial service. He'd written a personal note and asked Miles to post it for him—but he knew that a note wasn't the same as actually being there. It had felt horribly like a weak excuse.

And then the fallout from his own father's death had kept him on special leave from the army. For the last four months, Antonio Valenti had been kept busy supporting Luca as his brother took over the reins of ruling Casavalle. He'd also been helping with the preparations for both the coronation and Luca's upcoming wedding to Princess Meribel, the oldest daughter of King Jorge of the house of Asturias in the neighbouring kingdom of Aguilarez. He'd barely had a minute to himself since returning to Casavalle, so he'd let his unspoken promise to Nathan slide.

Though Antonio knew he should've *made* the time. Especially as he knew how bad Nathan had felt, leaving his sister to care for their mother while he'd joined the army at the age of sixteen so he could send money home to help them financially. He should've done more to help support his best friend's family. Been there for them, because he knew they had nobody else.

Tia had glanced back at him before going out on the balcony with an empty tray, presumably to collect glasses, but he had no idea whether or not she'd recognised him.

Then again, she was clearly working and her boss wouldn't be happy if she stood around chatting to guests at the charity gala when she was supposed to be clearing up. Given her family's circumstances, Antonio knew that Tia needed her job. It wouldn't be fair to risk her losing the job and having that added financial pressure, just to salve his own guilty conscience.

But he couldn't just leave things. Not now he'd seen her again. Surely she could spare him two minutes?

'Please excuse me. I'm expected to mingle,' he said to the guests he was with. As the patron of the charity, he was supposed to talk to every guest and thank them for their support; but he was pretty sure he'd already done that. So his conscience was clear as he headed towards the balcony where Tia had gone.

She was standing on the other side of the door as he opened it, and almost dropped her tray.

'Sorry,' he said. 'Tia. It's good to see you.'

'Thank you, Your Royal Highness,' she said

coolly. 'I would curtsey, but I'd rather avoid the risk of dropping my tray.'

He winced, knowing he deserved the rebuke. 'You don't need to curtsey, and it's Antonio to you. Your brother was my friend.'

'Yes, Your Royal Highness.'

Which put him very much in his place. He'd been a stranger and he deserved to be treated like one, despite his current attempt to be friendly with her. Given how he'd behaved, the last time they'd met, maybe it wasn't so surprising that she preferred to keep a barrier of formality against him. OK. He'd stick to formality.

'Ms Phillips,' he said. 'I appreciate that you're working right now, but perhaps we could talk when you've finished?'

'I really shouldn't be taking up guests' time, Your Royal Highness,' she said.

Which was a polite way of telling him he shouldn't be taking up her time, either. Another deserved rebuke, he thought. 'After your shift,' he said, glancing quickly at his watch. 'The gala finishes in five minutes.'

When it looked as if she was going to think up an excuse, he said softly, 'Please. It'd be so good to talk to someone who knew Nathan.'

* * *

For a moment, his brown eyes were filled with pain, before his expression returned to its former careful neutrality. So maybe the Prince wasn't quite as cold and uncaring as he'd seemed. That glimpse of pain just now told her that the Prince really *had* cared about her brother. Maybe she should cut the man some slack. Be kind to her brother's friend. Even though part of her still felt he should've made more of an effort, for her mum's sake.

'All right,' she said. 'I'll meet you when I'm done here. But I'm working tomorrow. I can't stay long.'

'Just a few minutes. Thank you.' He paused. 'I'm staying in the penthouse suite. I can of course arrange for a chaperone, if you prefer.'

'That won't be necessary, Your Royal Highness.' Like her brother, Prince Antonio was a man of honour. Tia knew without having to ask that his behaviour towards her would be respectful. 'The penthouse suite,' she echoed.

'My security team will let you in,' he said. 'Forgive me for being rude, but I'd better go back to the guests. I'm the patron of the charity.'

Meaning that he was here on official duties? Though the Prince had been so cold and starchy when he'd come to tell Tia and her mum the news about Nathan, she wasn't convinced he really cared about bereaved children, the way the patron would normally have a personal interest in the cause they supported. Though maybe losing his friend had taught him a little more empathy.

To her surprise, he held the door for her so she didn't have to struggle with her tray of glasses.

This was surreal.

She'd just made an assignation with a prince. In his penthouse suite.

A prince who'd been her brother's best friend, though because Nathan had kept his work and his family separate this was only the second time she'd ever met Prince Antonio. They didn't really know each other. The only thing they had in common was Nathan and the hole his death had left in their lives.

But maybe she should hear what he had to say. Maybe he'd give her some crumb of comfort she could give to her mum. That would be worth her feeling even more tired tomorrow morning.

The next few minutes passed in a blur of clearing tables and attending to the last-minute needs of guests, but finally she was done.

Sadie hugged her. 'Thanks so much for helping tonight, Tia. I owe you.'

'That's what friends are for,' Tia said with a smile. 'And you know it's a cause close to my heart.' She'd been in exactly the same position as the children that the charity helped.

'Get a taxi home. I'll pick up the bill,' Sadie said.

Tia shook her head. 'It's fine. I'll get the night tube. The walk will give me a chance to wind down.' After she'd met Prince Antonio. Not that she planned to tell her friend about *that*.

'Then I'm buying you dinner, some time this week. No arguments,' Sadie said.

'That would be good. Depending on how Mum is,' Tia added swiftly. No way was she going out if her mum was having a tough health day. Family came first.

'Or maybe I could bring dinner round for the three of us,' Sadie suggested.

'That might be nicer, if you don't mind. Mum

would really like that.' And the company would help to brighten her mum's day.

'Then we'll do it. Check your diary tomorrow and text me with your free dates,' Sadie said.

I'm free every day, Tia thought, but didn't say it. She was just grateful that one of her old school friends actually understood her situation enough to make the effort to stay in touch. Grace had encouraged her to make a life for herself; even though her grades hadn't been good enough for her to train as a teacher, Grace had suggested other ways into the classroom. Tia could work as a classroom assistant or at a playgroup, perhaps, or maybe she could do a foundation course at university and then do her degree and train as a teacher. But Tia hadn't wanted to leave her mum, knowing that Grace's health really wasn't good. Being away from home would've left her worrying that her mum was struggling, and eventually Tia had convinced her mother that she was much happier staying where she was.

'I will,' she promised.

Instead of leaving the hotel, Tia took the lift up to the penthouse suite. A man in a very ordinary suit leaned casually against the wall opposite the lifts as the doors opened, but Tia wasn't fooled; it was obvious that he was the Prince's security officer.

'Ms Phillips.' It was a statement, not a question. He clearly knew who she was and was expecting her. 'Would you like to come with me?'

It was a polite enough question, but she knew there wasn't a real choice. It was accompany him or go straight back down in the lift.

'Thank you,' she said.

He ushered her over to the door of the penthouse suite, and knocked. 'Your guest has arrived, sir.'

Not 'Your Royal Highness'? Or maybe he was from the Casavallian military.

'Thank you, Giacomo,' Antonio said as he opened the door. 'Please come in, Ms Phillips.'

The carpet was the sort that you sank into when you walked on it. One wall of the sitting room was pure glass, looking out over the Thames; it was late enough that the lights from the bridge and the buildings on the other bank were reflected on the dark water of the river.

'Thank you for coming. May I offer you a drink? Champagne?'

This was her cue to refuse politely and ask

him to just get on with it and see what he had to say. But since he had offered refreshment and she'd been on her feet all day and all evening...

'Actually, Your Royal Highness, I could really do with a cup of tea.'

'Of course.' He smiled then. 'You're very like your brother. At the end of the day, most of the team would relax with a cold beer. But Nathan said nothing could refresh you like a cup of tea.'

She could almost hear her brother's voice saying the words, and it put a lump in her throat.

'Strong enough to stand a spoon up in. One sugar. A dash of milk. And in a mug, not a cup,' he added.

That was when she knew for sure that he really had been close to Nathan. Because it was exactly what her brother would've said. And all of a sudden she felt a bit less wary of him.

'I remember,' she said, her breath catching.

'Do you take yours the same way?' he asked.

Normally she was just grateful if her tea was hot. 'Yes. Thank you, Your Royal Highness.'

And he actually made the mug of tea for her himself. No calling room service, no pretensions. Were princes supposed to be like this?

And, she noticed, he joined her in drinking tea. He didn't take sugar in his, though.

'Cheers,' he said, lifting his mug in a toast. 'To Nathan.'

She lifted her own mug. 'To Nathan.'

'You must miss him terribly. As do I.' He looked at her. 'I'm sorry I haven't kept in touch, Miss Phillips. Life is a little bit complicated at the moment.'

'Complicated?'

He shrugged. 'My father died not long after Nathan was killed. Obviously my older brother will be the one to succeed him, but there's a lot of political stuff to sort out.'

She'd had no idea that he'd lost his father, too. 'My condolences on the loss of your father, Your Royal Highness,' she said formally.

'Thank you. I know you've been in that situation.'

'Except I was ten when Dad died,' she said. 'He was killed in action, too.'

'That's tough for you,' he said. 'Losing your father and your brother the same way.'

'It's one of the reasons why I worked here tonight,' she said. 'I wanted to do my bit to help the charity.' To support children who'd been bereaved the way she had, because she knew what it felt like.

'You were a volunteer tonight?' He sounded surprised.

'Yes. Though, actually, my day job's in a café.' A proper Italian café, run by a middle-aged couple from Naples who'd taken her to their hearts and who always sent her home after her shift with treats for her mum.

'It's good of you to help. Thank you.' He paused. 'How is your mother?'

'Fine.' It wasn't strictly true, although thank-fully this week Grace was having a good patch where she was fully mobile and not quite as exhausted. Chronic fatigue syndrome was the kind of illness that had peaks and troughs, and Tia knew that a good week like this would be balanced out by one where her mother could barely get out of bed and would need a lot more help with day-to-day things.

'I'm sorry. I should've kept in touch.'

'Or come to his funeral.' The rebuke tumbled out before she could stop it.

He inclined his head. 'My apologies. I intended to be there. But I was called away on a mission, and it wasn't one that I could delegate to someone else.'

That hadn't occurred to her. It was a valid excuse, she supposed, though she still thought he could've sent her mother a personal note.

As if he'd guessed at what she was thinking, he said, 'I did write a letter to apologise for my absence.'

'Mum didn't get any letter from you.'

He frowned. 'I'm sorry it didn't arrive. I promise you, I did write.'

'It must've got lost in the post. That's not your fault.' Though he hadn't followed up on his note after his mission. Surely he could've found the time to at least call her mother?

He took a deep breath. 'What can I do to help?'

'Nothing,' she said immediately. They didn't need to lean on anyone. She and Grace were doing just fine on their own. They had their routines and they had good friends to support them. They didn't need a prince throwing money at them to salve his conscience.

'Nathan said you were proud and independent,' Antonio said gently. 'Which is a good thing. But your brother was part of my team.

My friend. And, despite what you must think, my team are like family to me. If I can help to make life easier, Miss Phillips, please let me know. Nathan wouldn't have wanted you to struggle.'

He was offering her a financial handout? She kept her temper with difficulty and said politely, 'Thank you, Your Royal Highness, but we're managing just fine as we are.'

'I didn't intend to offend you,' he said. 'Just...' For a moment, he looked racked with guilt. 'I couldn't do anything to save your brother.'

'It wasn't your fault that he was killed. And Nathan knew the risks of the job before he signed up for it.' She knew her brother had wanted to follow in their father's footsteps.

'I know. But it doesn't stop me missing him.'

Then he looked shocked, as if he hadn't meant to say that out loud.

And again that bleakness was back in his eyes for a moment before he managed to hide it again.

Prince Antonio, despite his privileged upbringing, seemed lonely, deep inside. Right now she'd been given a glimpse of the man behind the cool, collected mask. And she could almost hear her brother's voice echoing in her head: *He could do with a hug.*

Which would be way outside official protocol. Then again, some things were more important than protocol. So Tia put her mug on the coffee table, walked over to Prince Antonio, put his mug on the coffee table next to hers, and wrapped her arms around him.

For a long, long time, he just stood there, unmoving; but then, just as she was about to apologise and take a step backwards, he wrapped his arms around her and held her back, warm and comforting.

She really, really had intended it as comfort. *Just* comfort. Sharing their grief.

But one of them—she wasn't sure which of them—moved, and his cheek was pressed against hers. Her skin tingled where it touched his. Another tiny movement—hers? His?—and the corners of their mouths were touching.

The tingle spread.

Another infinitesimally small shift, and then his mouth was brushing against hers.

She shouldn't be doing this.

He was a prince and she was a waitress. Their lives were so far apart, it was untrue. Neither of them was in a position to start any kind of relationship. He had official duties and she was busy working and looking after her mother. Nothing could possibly come of this.

But the temptation to take comfort from him and to comfort him in turn was so strong.

Maybe this was something they both needed. Just for one night. No strings.

Because, just as Antonio had shown no emotion when he'd come to tell them the news about Nathan, Tia had locked her own tears away because she'd needed to be strong for her mother.

When he broke the kiss and looked into her eyes, she could see the tears glittering there, the emotion he was trying so hard to repress.

Maybe tonight they could cry together. Find a release together. Comfort each other. *Heal* each other.

Just for tonight.

'Stay with me, Tia?' he whispered.

Common sense said that she should leave. She was due at work tomorrow morning. And there was her mother to think about.

But Becky was only next door if she was needed. Tia could drink coffee tomorrow rather than tea to get her through her shift. Right now, Antonio needed her—and she needed him.

She laid her palm against his cheek. 'Yes.'

He kissed her again, scooped her into his arms and carried her to his bed.

CHAPTER ONE

November

THERE WAS NO other way round it, Tia thought, curving a protective hand around her bump.

Miles Montague, the palace secretary, had been perfectly polite to her just now. But, just as he'd done with every single one of her previous calls, he'd rebuffed her, refusing to put her through to Antonio. She'd begged him to pass on a message, asking Antonio to call her. She'd told Miles that she knew the Prince, and it was really important that she speak to him.

But Miles had left her with the impression that, as an eligible bachelor, Prince Antonio had hundreds of women calling, claiming they 'knew' him because they had shaken his hand once or attended an event where he was on the guest list. The palace secretary clearly thought she was just another in a long line of unwanted callers, and he wasn't going to put her through.

Miles had been kind enough. He'd asked her if he could help. He'd asked her to tell him what the problem was.

But how could she let news like *this* go through a third party, no matter how discreet he seemed or how well he knew Antonio? This was something she needed to tell the Prince herself. That their one night together, the night that was supposed to give them both comfort and never be referred to again, had had consequences.

She'd tried to explain that Antonio knew her brother; but Miles had asked in that kind but immovable way exactly *how* Antonio knew her brother, and she'd ended up in tears of frustration.

How could the palace secretary not even know the names of the people who were on Antonio's team in the international alliance? Surely he'd know information like that?

Frustrated and miserable, she'd ended the call.

She'd tried a dozen times now to talk to Antonio, to tell him about the baby.

And failed a dozen times, too.

She didn't have his email address, and even

if she did she suspected that someone else—probably Miles Montague, or one of his team—would check through the messages before they reached Antonio, weeding out the ones they judged unimportant or inappropriate, which would definitely include hers. The same would go for letters. Any message she left would be blocked just as effectively as her phone calls had been blocked.

It left her with no other alternative. She'd have to go to Casavalle herself to tell him about the baby. Face to face.

If she sat on Antonio's doorstep and refused to budge, they'd have to let her talk to him. And she could tell him the news—well, as she was six months pregnant, he'd be able to see that quite well enough for himself, she thought wryly—and then leave.

Originally, she hadn't intended to tell him at all. She hadn't realised for a couple of months that she was pregnant; then, when she'd finally realised her period was a lot later than usual and did a test, she'd seen the centre spread in the celebrity magazine she'd bought for her mum as a treat. A story about Prince Antonio of Casavalle, speculating which of the four women who'd graced his arm that month might be his future bride.

How ironic. Tia had thought she'd had a glimpse of the real Prince, the man her brother had been friends with—but maybe he was exactly what the media said he was. He hadn't really needed her to comfort him, that night, because he had strings of women ready to comfort him. And she'd been so angry at herself for being a fool that it had taken her mum another month to talk her round into telling Antonio about her pregnancy.

Six weeks later, she still hadn't told him—though not for the want of trying.

She grimaced. She didn't expect anything from him, either for herself or for the baby, and she certainly wasn't looking for a cash handout or anything like that. Antonio had been her brother's friend, and she owed it to him to tell him that the baby existed. And that was the limit of their obligations to each other, because their lives were too different for anything else to happen.

She flicked into the Internet. The cheapest flight to Casavalle would get her in at about half-past eight tomorrow evening. She had no idea how far it was from the airport to the palace, but even though she wouldn't have to wait to collect her luggage she would still have to go through airport security and customs. Maybe she'd get to the palace at ten p.m.—which was way too late for anyone to be admitted to the palace offices.

To get there for the early afternoon… She scanned the flight schedules. She'd have to leave London really early in the morning and change planes at Rome, and she'd have a two-hour layover in between. Plus the flight was a lot more expensive. It was money she could really do with elsewhere in her budget; but if she got the cheaper flight and stayed at a hotel overnight, it would cost even more, and she couldn't waste money that she needed to spend on the baby.

She stroked her bump. 'Hopefully we'll find somewhere quiet to sit at the airport, and we'll get a taxi from the airport to the palace.' She'd ask to speak to Miles Montague. And as soon as he saw her he'd realise exactly why it was so important for her to talk to Antonio. Then she could deliver her message—and go home.

* * *

Wednesday. 'Hump day', they called it in civilian jobs. The middle of the week.

Except you didn't get a day off from being a prince, Antonio thought.

And you particularly didn't get a day off when you had a long-lost older sister who was very probably going to be the one taking their father's place as the ruler of the kingdom, and an older brother whose fiancée had told him on the eve of their wedding that she was pregnant with her true love's baby, resulting in the royal wedding that the whole country had been looking forward to being cancelled at the last minute. The Asturias family were just as keen as the Valentis to minimise the scandal, so they'd issued a joint statement to the media that the wedding had been cancelled due to 'irreconcilable differences' between the bride and groom.

Luca, wanting to get away from the palace, had gone to meet their long-lost half-sister Gabriella in Canada; which meant that, instead of their original plan of Antonio being the one to go over and meet Gabriella, he was stuck here.

In charge of the country.

Something he'd never really expected to happen, despite being third in line to the throne. He'd thought his father would go on for ever, and then Luca would take over, and then Luca and Princess Meribel would have children who would be next in line.

But, this last year, their lives had been turned upside down. Everything he'd thought he knew turned out not to be true.

Life at the palace was turning out to be much more stressful than taking part in dangerous missions in the army. At least as a soldier Antonio had known what he was doing. He'd had a strategy. He'd had a team he could rely on. They were all working on the same side; his team listened to him, as their leader, and he'd had a brilliant second-in-command in Nathan. In Casavalle, things were nowhere near as clear cut. It was so easy to misinterpret words and put the wrong spin on things; the most innocent comment could swiftly turn into a political nightmare.

Just one day, he thought wistfully. He'd love to have just one single day where he could have the time to gather his thoughts instead of constantly firefighting and dealing with political situations. Had it been like that for their father?

Was that why King Vincenzo had always been so remote and distant, even from his sons, because he'd simply been worn out from watching every single word or expression or gesture?

At the rap on his open door, Antonio looked up to see the palace secretary standing there.

'Good afternoon, Miles. What can I do for you?' he asked, forcing a smile and hoping that whatever the secretary wanted from him wasn't going to mean yet more politics and media attention.

'Sir,' Miles began.

The palace secretary was usually unflappable. Right now he looked distinctly nervous and Antonio's heart sank. Was the palace about to be hit with yet another scandal? They said things came in threes, and a long-lost princess and a broken engagement because the bride was pregnant by someone else definitely counted as two...

This felt like living in a television soap opera. And Antonio wasn't enjoying the drama one little bit. Yet again, he wished he was back in the army. Back in the job he was really good at.

'What is it?' he asked.

'I have someone asking to see you.'

Why would Miles be worried about that? 'Who?' he asked, narrowing his eyes.

'A young lady. Tia Phillips. She said she knows you.'

Tia was here?

Antonio shook himself mentally and damped down that little frisson of desire. Their one night together wasn't going to be repeated. They'd both made it clear that it was for comfort, it was for one night only, and neither of them had any expectations of the other. And Miles didn't need to know anything about that. He just needed to know that Tia was telling the truth. 'Yes, she knows me. I served with her brother.'

Guilt flooded through Antonio. In a way, he'd abandoned Tia twice, now—the first time after he'd told her that her brother had been killed, because he hadn't known how to deal with it; then he'd been called back to work, and after that his father had died and he'd been busy with official duties. The second time had been that night in London following the charity gala, when they'd ended up comforting each other in bed. Tia had vanished early the next morning before he'd awoken, leaving him a note explaining that she was due at work.

Which had pretty much let him off the hook.

Part of him had felt relieved, because it meant he didn't have to unpick his feelings and deal with them; but part of him had felt guilty about sleeping with his best friend's little sister. It had been mutual comfort, but he still felt responsible. And he'd planned to call her to see if there was anything he could do to help her mother. He wasn't that much of a cad, no matter that the media liked to call him a playboy who would never settle down. The only true bit about the media's claims was that he didn't want to settle down; he kept his love affairs short and very discreet. And he always made it very clear that he wasn't offering his girlfriends a future. That the relationship was just for now, not for ever.

But, as he'd been about to call Tia, that morning, his mother had called him with the news about Gabriella and her potential claim to the throne. Queen Maria had needed her youngest son to come home to discuss the situation with her and help her to plan what they should do next; and it would all have to be done confidentially because she hadn't wanted to put the extra pressure on Luca, who they both thought had quite enough on his plate ruling the country. All thoughts of Tia had flown out of his head and he'd gone straight back to Casavalle without getting in touch with her.

Antonio and the Queen had been close to working out how to deal with the situation about Gabriella when Princess Meribel dropped her bombshell and Luca's wedding was cancelled. Everything had gone haywire after that, and in the last month Antonio felt as if he'd barely had a moment to breathe.

'She's telephoned the palace a few times,' Miles said, 'but I didn't expect her to turn up here.'

Tia had called a few times? Why? 'Why didn't you put her through?' Antonio asked.

Miles winced. 'I didn't want to repeat the mistake I made with Gabriella's letter to Queen Maria.'

Gabriella's letter. The bombshell that had made it through to the Queen because it was marked 'Personal and Confidential'. Luca had been quite hard on the palace secretary about it, and Miles had been extremely vigilant about which messages made it through to the family ever since.

But Antonio was the youngest child, and he was pretty sure he was more approachable than his father had been—or even his elder brother. And surely Miles had known him for long enough to realise that Antonio wouldn't go all cold and icy on him if he made a mistake? Things happened unexpectedly; you just had to deal with them efficiently and effectively as they came up.

'And now she's here, wanting to see you,' Miles continued.

Antonio smiled, wanting to reassure the secretary. 'That's fine. As I said, I worked with her brother. He was a good friend. I can spare a few minutes to talk to her. Where is she?'

'In my office,' Miles said. 'But, sir, before you go to meet her, you need to know that she's making some quite outlandish claims. She says she's six months pregnant—and she says the baby is yours.'

'She *what*?' Antonio felt as if someone had just winded him.

'She's pregnant. Very pregnant.' Miles winced. 'You can see the baby moving in her stomach.'

Antonio counted back in his head. May. They'd slept together in May.

And now it was November.

Six months.

Antonio was pretty sure that this wasn't a situation like his brother's, where Princess Meribel had been at the point of possibly passing off another man's baby as Luca's. Nathan had been proud of his little sister, proud of her independence and her loyalty and her resourcefulness. Antonio believed that Tia wouldn't lie about something like this.

Plus the timing fitted exactly.

'But of course the baby can't be yours,' Miles said.

Oh, yes, it could.

Six months.

Tia must've known she was pregnant for at least three of those months, probably more. Why on earth hadn't she said anything to him before?

Then again, Miles had said she'd called a few times but he hadn't put her through. Clearly Tia *had* tried to talk to him and she'd been gently put aside by the palace secretary.

'How long has she been trying to get in touch with me?' Antonio asked.

'A few weeks,' Miles admitted.

So she must've tried to tell him almost as soon as she knew about the baby, then. If Miles had been stonewalling her for weeks, coming here must've been the last resort for her because she'd had no other way to get in touch with him—apart from going to the media and causing his family maximum embarrassment, and that just didn't fit with what he knew of Nathan's little sister.

'I spoke to Prince Luca about it,' Miles continued, 'and he agreed it was most likely she'd seen your photograph in a magazine, decided she was in love with you and made up a story to—'

'Hang on. *Luca* knew about this?' Antonio cut in.

'That she'd called you. Not about the baby.' Miles squirmed. 'I only found out about that today, when I saw her. The bump is, um, quite noticeable.'

Antonio groaned. 'We'll discuss this later. Luca, too. But I need to see her. Now.'

'You mean she's telling the truth, sir?'

'Yes,' Antonio said grimly, the guilt he felt at sleeping with his friend's little sister intensifying by the second. Not only had he slept with her, he'd made her pregnant. 'The timing matches up, so I'm pretty sure the baby's mine.' And he sprinted out of the room towards Miles's office.

Tia felt sick—and it was nothing to do with her pregnancy and everything to do with the situation. What *had* she been thinking, coming here? Now Miles Montague had left her in his office, her surroundings sank in. She was in a palace—a *palace*, for pity's sake. People like her didn't go to palaces, not unless they were visiting a stately home or museum while on holiday. This was surreal.

And just how was Antonio going to react to the news? With shock? Dismay? Horror? She'd told herself all the way here that his reaction didn't matter, that she'd deliver the news and walk away—but it *did* matter, now she was here. And a tiny, very foolish part of her couldn't help hoping that he'd be thrilled to see her and would sweep her into his arms...

Of course that wasn't going to happen. She

was six months pregnant, and he certainly wouldn't try to lift her. And this was his territory. He'd be every inch the cold, snooty Prince who'd told her that her brother had been killed.

Right on cue, Antonio strolled into the room, all cool and calm and unruffled. He didn't even bat an eyelash or look remotely shocked; just as she'd guessed, he was totally cold. And that tiny, daft bit of her that had been hoping for the impossible simply shrivelled and died.

Worst of all, the flare of attraction she'd felt towards him was still there. Stronger, if anything, now she knew what it felt like to spend the night in his arms. Even seeing him made her heart feel as if it was doing a somersault.

How stupid was she? He was a prince and she was a waitress. The stories about Cinderella, Snow White, and Beauty and the Beast were just that: fairy stories to entertain children. This was real life; and her life was about as opposite from Antonio's as it was possible to get. They didn't have a future together.

'Good to see you, Tia,' he said.

Was it? His face was so unreadable, she didn't have a clue.

'I trust Miles has offered you some refreshment?' he asked.

'Yes.' And she'd refused. All she'd wanted was to see Antonio, deliver her message and leave so she could catch her plane home. Now she was here, she *really* wanted to leave.

He looked at the clear desk in front of her and frowned. 'I'll organise some tea. That is, assuming you can drink tea?'

She knew what he was referring to; but she was well past the morning sickness stage. 'Thank you, but no thank you. I'm not staying.'

He said nothing, simply tipped his head slightly to one side to indicate that he was listening to whatever she had to say. He looked every inch a prince, and incredibly remote and forbidding.

She lifted her chin. 'I just came to let you know the situation.'

'That you're six months pregnant, according to Miles. You could have—'

Told him? OK, so she'd waited a month, not wanting to talk to the Playboy Prince. But for the six weeks since her mother had persuaded her to talk to him, she'd been trying, and it stung that he was making her feel as if *she* was the bad guy. 'I tried,' she cut in quietly. 'I rang the palace. More than once, actually. But I didn't want to leave a message about this. I wanted to tell you myself. Mr Montague wouldn't put me through to you when I called. In case you'd lost my number, I left it again. But, as you didn't call me back, I assumed he didn't tell you that I'd called.'

She didn't have a clue about how he was reacting to this. Was he shocked, angry, horrified? This man had inscrutability down to a fine art.

'It meant that coming to tell you in person was my only option. So now you know.'

He hadn't made a single move towards her. That night in London… Well, obviously Antonio had drawn a line under that, a long time ago. They both had. Neither of them had expected consequences. Although she'd left him that note, and a tiny bit of her had hoped that he'd call her, she hadn't really expected him to do anything. That night was what it was. A one-night stand.

Then the reality of it hit her. She'd assumed that Miles Montague hadn't passed on the message. Maybe he *had* given Prince Antonio the message, but the Prince simply hadn't wanted to return her call. How could she have been so stupid?

She clearly wasn't wanted here, and neither was the baby.

Though she'd expected Antonio not to want to know, she'd had time to get used to the idea of being a single mum. She'd cope. Coping was what she'd done every day since Nathan had left to join the army and she'd become her mother's sole carer at the age of thirteen. She'd find a way to juggle motherhood, a job and continuing to care for her mum. Giovanni and Vittoria, her bosses at the café, were kind and sympathetic. It would be fine.

She suppressed the memories that had rushed into her head when Antonio had walked into the room—the surge of desire, the memory of the way his skin had felt against hers, his strength combined with surprising gentleness. Although this man was the father of her baby, she had to remember that first and foremost he was a prince—and her feelings towards him were completely inappropriate, as well as completely unwanted by him.

She didn't even know what to call him.

Your Royal Highness? Prince Antonio?

Considering that they'd spent the night together...

It was all too much for her. She didn't want to stay in this cold, formal palace a minute longer than she had to. She wanted to leave. *Now.* 'Excuse me. I have a flight to catch.' She stood up, gathered her coat under her arm and turned away.

Antonio reached out and touched her shoulder, gently making her turn to face him again. 'Tia. Please stay. We need to talk.'

Even though there was soft cotton between his skin and hers, the contact was enough to stir up old memories, making her skin tingle. Which was completely inappropriate, and it made her feel so out of sorts that she snapped, 'There's nothing to talk about.'

His gaze flicked down to her bump and up to her face again. 'I rather think there is.'

'Look, I'm not expecting anything from you. I haven't come here looking for financial support or anything like that. I'm not planning to sell an exclusive to the gossip columns. I just thought you had a right to know about the baby's existence, that's all.'

'Thank you for telling me. And I'm sorry that the palace made it difficult for you to get in touch with me.'

So was she. But, when she thought about it, she could kind of understand it. 'You're a prince. For all they knew, I could've been some crazed stalker.'

'You're the sister of my best friend,' Antonio said.

And the mother of his child. Though he hadn't said as much.

'And yet again I owe you an apology. I seem to be making a habit of not contacting you.'

He could say that again.

He'd done it twice now. She wasn't setting herself up for a third mistake, where Antonio Valenti was concerned. How did the saying go? Fool me once, shame on you. Fool me twice, shame on me.

She'd been quite enough of a fool. Though at least he wasn't offering some flimsy excuse. On the other hand, a simple 'sorry' might have been nice. He'd said he owed her an apology, but he hadn't actually given her an apology, had he?

'Tia, please stay. I'm still in the middle of

processing the fact that I'm going to be a father,' he said. 'And we have a lot to talk about. But, first, I'm going to organise that cup of tea. And you've come all the way from London, so I'm guessing you haven't had anything to eat.'

'I had a sandwich on the plane.' Half a sandwich. It had made her feel sick. Or maybe that had been nerves at the idea of coming here to tell Antonio about the baby.

'Airline food,' Antonio said, 'isn't the most wonderful.'

'I don't want to bother your kitchen staff.'

He smiled. 'You won't be bothering them. Come to my apartment. I'll make you a mug of tea and a sandwich myself. Or pasta.' He spread his hands. 'Or whatever it is you'd like to eat.'

She blinked at him, trying to take it in. He was offering to make her some food? Seriously? 'But princes don't cook.'

'They do if they're in the army,' he said. 'If they want their team to respect them, they take their turn doing everything. And I mean everything. I've done my share of cleaning duties, too.'

'Oh.' She really hadn't expected that. Even

though he'd made her a mug of tea himself, that night in London.

'Come with me,' he said. 'And I'll carry your bags.'

'I don't have any luggage. I have a seat on the late flight back to London via Rome, tonight,' she said. 'I only came to tell you about the baby. I wasn't planning to stay.'

'Don't go. Please.' He blew out a breath. 'We really do have a lot to talk about. I don't know if you've followed the news about Casavalle, but an awful lot has been going on here. It's wall-to-wall scandal sheet stuff. The media is going to take one look at you, rub their hands with glee and start digging for more scandal.'

She hadn't thought of that. 'But they don't know why I'm here.'

'They'll speculate. It doesn't matter whether it's true or not. They'll suggest whatever gives them the most readers. They'll talk to anyone who knows you and dredge up any hint of scandal. Your mother is going to be a sitting target for them. From now until at least when the baby's born, you're all going to need my protection,' he continued. 'Which includes the help of Miles Montague. And, as you know, almost nothing gets through Miles. Even when sometimes it should.'

There was a rap on the office door.

'Yes,' Antonio said.

The palace secretary himself opened the door to his office. 'Sir? Miss Phillips? Is everything all right?' he asked, looking concerned.

'It will be,' Antonio said. 'Miles, I'll brief you properly later. But for now this isn't to be discussed anywhere or with anyone—and that includes my mother, Luca and Gabriella.'

There was a slight note of warning in his tone, and the older man flushed as he walked over to his desk. 'Of course, sir.'

Antonio sighed. 'I'll talk to them when I'm ready,' he said, and this time his voice was a little gentler. 'If anyone needs me urgently in the next hour or so, we'll be in my apartment. But I'd appreciate it if you could stall anyone if possible, Miles. Tia and I really need to talk in private and without interruptions.'

'Of course. If you need anything…'

Antonio patted his shoulder. 'You're there. I know. And I'm grateful for that.'

Miles nodded, then looked at Tia, his expression awkward. 'I apologise, Miss Phillips, for earlier. When you called the office, and when you first came here.'

It had upset her, but she could understand why he'd acted that way. 'You were doing your job,' she said. 'Protecting the Prince.'

'And Tia's going to be under your protection now, too,' Antonio said. 'I'll brief you shortly. Tia, come with me.' He looked at her and added swiftly, 'Please.'

Good. Because she wasn't Antonio's subject or his employee, and she wasn't going to let him order her about.

The palace had seemed daunting enough from the outside: a massive white stone building with towers and turrets and spires and huge windows; a long driveway lined with enormous Norway spruces covered alternately with blue and white lights; and huge entrance doors at the top of the sweeping granite steps. Tia had found the interior even more daunting, with the enormous foyer that felt more like a cathedral space, with a Christmas tree that had to be a good forty feet tall; the angel on top was close to touching the ceiling, and it was beautifully decorated with what looked like priceless one-of-a-kind baubles, one of which seemed to be in a special display. Crowds actually came in to the palace to see the tree, which was how Tia had managed to slip in and ask to see the palace secretary in the first place.

It was magnificent. But it was also very formal, and it didn't leave her with the warmth she felt with their own Christmas tree back in London, with its decorations that had been collected year after year by her mother and every single one of them had meaning and memories. Their rather threadbare artificial Christmas tree didn't go up until the week before Christmas; here, it was early November and already everything was in its place. Then again, she supposed, things were different with the public rooms of a palace; visitors would expect to see decorations on display this early.

Behind the beautiful garlands of fir and pine on the mantels and staircases, the rooms were richly decorated, with cream walls and lots of gold everywhere. There were huge windows, large mirrors that reflected the light back from the windows and the crystal and gold chandeliers and made the rooms seem even more massive, ceilings covered with priceless paintings, Christmas trees in every room whose decorations she suspected had been put in place with a ruler measuring the precise distance between each one, enormous exotic poinsettias gracing side tables, sweeping staircases leading into long corridors, luxurious carpets you literally sank into as you walked on them...

It was another world, one where the likes of Tia could never fit in.

And it was overwhelming.

Tia was aware that Antonio was talking to her as he ushered her up the sweeping staircase to his first-floor apartment, but she couldn't concentrate on what he was saying. All she could see was the regal magnificence of their surroundings, and it left her feeling more and more out of place.

Finally he opened a door and indicated to her to enter.

His sitting room was much more ordinary than the rest of the palace. The furniture here didn't look too antique and too priceless to touch, let alone sit on, and to her relief there was much less gold in evidence. There were photographs on the mantelpiece in what looked like solid gold frames, mainly of what she assumed was Antonio's family; but there were also photographs of Antonio's team in the army, and tears pricked her eyelids when she recognised her brother among them.

'Let me get you that tea,' Antonio said, ushering her into the kitchen—a sizeable room by normal standards, but thankfully smaller than the rooms she'd seen so far in the palace.

'Thank you. That would be nice.'

'What would you like to eat?'

She shook her head. 'Thank you, but I'm not really hungry.'

He gave her a speaking look. 'You're pregnant. You need to eat.'

She didn't reply but, a couple of minutes later, she found herself sitting at his kitchen table with a mug of tea made just how she liked it and a chicken salad sandwich.

'I really didn't expect you to—' she began.

'Eat,' he cut in. 'Then we'll talk.'

It left her with no choice but to follow his instructions. And she had to admit that the sandwich and the mug of tea did make her feel better. He didn't say a word until she'd finished, simply sipped his tea.

And then he looked at her. 'OK. So, first off,' he said gently, 'how are you?'

'I'm fine.'

'*Really* fine? Because I know some women have a tough time in pregnancy.'

She shrugged. 'I had a bit of morning sickness in the early weeks. Nothing out of the usual.' She opened her handbag, took out a photograph and handed it to him. 'I wanted to give you this.'

'Thank you,' he said politely.

'It's our baby. From the twenty-week scan, last month.'

'Our baby,' he echoed.

She still had absolutely no idea what he was thinking, what he was feeling. His voice and his face were completely expressionless as he looked at the photograph. On the surface he was all urbane charm, just as a prince should be. But was he shocked? Horrified? Secretly pleased? She didn't have a clue. Who was the real man behind the royal facade?

'So,' he said. 'I'll ask you the difficult question first. Do you plan to keep the baby?'

'It's way too late for a termination.' Not that she'd wanted that, in any case.

'I didn't mean that. Were you planning to give the baby up for adoption after the birth?'

'No.'

'So you're keeping him. Or her.'

Not 'it'. She was grateful that at least he hadn't said *that*. 'Yes.'

'Then I have financial responsibilities towards you.'

'That isn't why I came. I can manage.' It would be a struggle, but she was used to that. She'd muddle through, the way she always had, working whatever hours she could fit in around the baby and her mum.

'Tia, this is a Valenti baby,' he said. 'There are expectations. If nothing else, this baby...' He sucked in a breath. 'The way things stand, this baby could be fourth in line to the throne.'

She looked at him in shock. 'What? How?'

'It's been a bit complicated around here. Which is why I didn't get in touch with you after... London.'

The night they'd spent together.

The night that clearly hadn't meant anything to him.

The night that had resulted in their baby.

'Uh-huh,' she said, in an attempt to be as cool and calm and collected as he seemed, though inside she wanted to yell at him.

'You left me that note and I fully intended to call you later that day, after your shift,' Antonio said. 'But, that morning, my mother called me to tell me about Gabriella—my father's daughter from his first marriage, except none of us had any idea she even existed until quite recently. My mother needed to talk to me about it and help her decide how to deal with the situation. She wanted to talk to me because Luca already had enough on his plate, ruling the country and preparing to be King. I had to come straight back to Casavalle, because my family needed me.'

Tia could understand that. It was the same for her and for Nathan: they'd been there for their mother because she was their family and she needed them.

'And I'm afraid my mind was so focused on the situation at home, I didn't think to contact you. I'm sorry.'

Tia had been hurt when Antonio hadn't been in touch after the charity gala, even though she knew she was being ridiculous about it: of course a prince wasn't going to fall for a mere waitress. Of course he wanted nothing more from her than their night of passion. It had been a one-off thing. But now she was seeing things from a different perspective. Antonio was part of a much bigger picture.

'At the moment we're waiting for DNA results, but my mother, Luca and I all think it's very probable that Gabriella is indeed the oldest child of our father, which means she's entitled to accede to the throne and rule Casavalle. She has no children, which makes my brother Luca her heir and puts him second in line to the throne. Luca also has no children; although Princess Meribel, his former fiancée, is pregnant, the baby isn't Luca's. So that makes me Luca's heir and third in line to the throne; and that means our baby is my heir and fourth in line to the throne.' He shrugged. 'Though if we're wrong about the DNA test or Gabriella decides not to accede to the throne, then everything shifts up one place and our baby will be third in line.'

It hadn't really hit home until that moment, but Tia realised right then that her baby was of royal blood.

A baby in line for a crown.

'I...' She tailed off, hardly able to take in the enormity of the situation.

'As I said,' Antonio continued quietly, 'it's been a little complicated around here. Luca's wedding to Meribel has been planned for a very long time. But Meribel told Luca on the eve of their wedding that she was in love with someone else and was pregnant with his baby, so she couldn't go through with marrying him. We agreed with her family that we'd say the wedding was cancelled due to irreconcilable differences, though the people of Aguilarez—Meribel's kingdom, on the other side of the mountains—assumed that meant Luca had practically jilted her at the altar, and they blamed him for the wedding not happening.

'It was politically...' He grimaced. 'Let's just say it was a bit sensitive. If we didn't tell the truth, it could lead to a great deal of discord between our countries. Yet if we told the truth—that Meribel was the one to have the affair—then it would be putting the blame on her, and that would be dishonourable.'

Tia didn't quite understand that. 'How could it be dishonourable when *she* was the one who had the affair?'

'It's still dishonourable,' Antonio insisted.

'So whatever you did, you'd lose,' Tia said slowly.

'Something like that. Except then someone leaked the truth of the matter. Not from our side,' he was quick to clarify. 'Meribel is in hiding right now, and it feels as if the media has put Casavalle under a microscope, scrutinising every move any of us makes and spotting every potential scandal.' He looked at her. 'Someone in the palace will have noticed you, and they will have heard you ask to speak to Miles. They will definitely have noticed your bump. So people will be asking questions about you—who are you, and why did you want to speak to the palace secretary? Whose baby are you carrying? They'll be watching for you to leave the palace.

'And the paparazzi don't play nice, Tia. They'll strike up a conversation at the airport and you'll think you're simply chatting to another passenger to pass the time. They'll ask all kinds of questions and pump you for information without you even knowing what they're doing, and the next thing you know it'll be all over the media. They'll dig on the Internet and they'll know everything about you before you get back to London—where you live, where you work, all about your mother's health. They'll follow you and they'll doorstep you.'

'Doorstep me?' She didn't understand.

'They'll wait outside your front door in a gaggle. The back door, too. There's no escape from them. The second you open any door, the flashbulbs will go off and they'll be yelling your name and asking you questions. If you've ever seen it happen in a film, I can assure you that it's been romanticised. In real life, it's much harsher. You have to push your way through the mob, and all the time there will be microphones shoved in your face and flashbulbs going off and people yelling.

'If you say anything, it'll be spun to suit their agenda. If you say nothing, then they'll speculate, and they'll do it with the nastiest implications—and you won't be able to protest because they'll claim they're asking questions, not making a statement. Your life won't be your own.'

That hadn't occurred to her. She'd simply thought to let Antonio know that their night together had had consequences, then quietly go back to London. 'I... Look, if there's a way you can get me from the palace to the airport without them seeing me, then I promise not to talk to a single person until I'm back home with my mum.'

He shook his head. 'It's already too late for that. As I said, things have been complicated around here lately.'

And she'd just added another complication to his life. An illegitimate baby.

Her misery must've shown in her expression, because he took her hand. 'Tia. I know neither of us planned this. But you have my support now and you definitely need my protection. I think we both need to get our heads round the situation, and the middle of a royal palace isn't the best place to do that. I know somewhere quiet we can go for a few days that will give us a chance to think things through and talk about the future.'

'But I wasn't planning to stay here, not even for a night. I don't have even a toothbrush with me, let alone any clean clothes,' Tia protested. 'And my mum's expecting me back home tonight.'

'Then call her. Tell her that you're staying here for a little while.' He paused. 'Give me three days, Tia.'

'Three *days*?' Tia was horrified. 'What if Mum needs me?'

'Do you have a neighbour or a friend nearby who can keep an eye out for her?' Antonio asked. 'Or I can arrange for a nurse to come in and help her, if you prefer.' He looked at her. 'I apologise. Nathan didn't tell me much about your mother's condition, other than that she'd been poorly since you were small. And I was brought up not to ask personal questions. So I'm afraid I don't know how ill she is.'

'Mum has chronic fatigue syndrome,' Tia said. 'It used to be called ME—myalgic en-cephalomyelitis.'

When Antonio looked blank, she continued, 'After Dad was killed in action, Mum went down with a virus, and we think that's what triggered the CFS because she never really recovered. It's a bit like having the flu, with joint pains and a headache you simply can't shift, and absolute exhaustion—but it doesn't go away after a couple of weeks, like the flu does. She has it all the time. So she needs to rest a lot.

'It's a variable condition; some days she's fine and to look at her you'd never know she was ill, and other days she can barely get out of bed. And she's *not* lazy or stupid. It's not like when you're feeling just a bit tired after a busy day—she gets absolutely exhausted and physically can't do anything. If she has a day when she's feeling really well and overdoes things, then she'll really pay for it for a few days afterwards. She has to be careful.'

'And you look after her?'

'Yes, and I don't begrudge a second of it. I love her. She's my mum.' Growing up, Tia had had days when she'd wished her life had been more like that of her friends, where she'd had time to do homework and hang out with her friends and meet boys, instead of struggling to keep up with her studies and worrying that her mum's condition was getting worse, and never starting a relationship because she knew it couldn't go anywhere. But she'd done her best to hide it from her mother, because she loved Grace and didn't want her mother to feel as if she was a burden.

Grace had encouraged her to go out with her friends, but Tia didn't like leaving her mum, except when she went to work and she was only just round the corner and could rush back if there was an emergency.

'Tia,' he said gently, 'we're going to need to talk about the best way to support your mother when you have a small baby to look after as well. Because you're not going to be able to do everything.'

Oh, yes, she could. She always had. 'It'll be fine.' She lifted her chin. 'I'll manage. We always do.'

Meaning that she'd struggle and drive herself into the ground.

Antonio was shocked by the sheer protectiveness he felt towards her. And it wasn't just because she was his best friend's little sister. There was something about Tia Phillips. She was brave and strong and independent, not looking for the easy way out—she'd been very explicit that she expected nothing from him. He admired her courage; yet, at the same time, he wanted to take some of those burdens away. What she'd just told him, in addition to the little that Nathan had let slip, made him realise that she must've spent most of her life looking after her mother. She'd never really had a normal childhood.

Well, she didn't have to struggle any more. He could support her. Though he was pretty sure that her pride would get in the way and she'd refuse any help. So he needed to gain her trust, first. And that meant being specific rather than vague.

'Come with me to my house in the mountains for three days,' he said. 'Let's give ourselves a bit of time to adjust to the situation, and then we can talk about the baby.'

She looked torn. 'It depends on how Mum is.'

'Call her,' he said. 'Talk to her. See what she thinks. I'll give you some space. I'll be in the sitting room when you're ready.'

'Thank you,' she said.

He left her to it, and went into his sitting room. Babies. This was the third baby shock in a row for the palace: first Gabriella's mother being pregnant and never telling her ex-husband, King Vincenzo, about the baby and running away without telling him; then Princess Meribel's affair ending in her being pregnant by another man; and now Tia expecting a baby after their one night together.

The media would have a field day. And, although he had the resources to ride out the storm, Tia was vulnerable.

There was only one solution to this.

But he didn't think it was going to be an easy solution. He was going to have to tread very carefully indeed.

Grace Phillips answered on the third ring.

'How are you, Mum?' Tia asked.

'I'm fine,' Grace said, a little too quickly for Tia's liking. 'Did you get to see Prince Antonio?'

'I did.' She sighed. 'Mum, he wants me to stay for a few days—three days, he said. He wants to talk things over.'

'That's a good idea,' Grace said.

'But I don't want to leave you on your own.'

'I'm fine, love. Really. Becky's next door if I need anything.'

'But that was just for today. I can't ask her to keep an eye out for you for three whole days.'

'You don't have to. I'll ask her,' Grace said. 'And I'm not overdoing things, before you start worrying. I can manage.'

Tia wasn't so sure. 'But what if you have a bad day tomorrow?'

'Then Becky will help,' Grace said. 'You need to talk to Prince Antonio, for the baby's sake. And for yours.'

'Mum, I...'

'I know he's from a different world,' Grace said gently, 'but Nathan always said he was a good man. Listen to what he has to say.'

'But I can't stay here. I haven't got any clean clothes with me, or even a toothbrush.' This was ridiculous. Tia was used to being independent, sorting things out. Their financial circumstances had taught her to be resourceful. So why did she suddenly feel like bursting into tears?

Maybe that fish-out-of-water feeling showed in her voice, because Grace said, 'I'm sure someone at the palace will be able to lend you something to wear, and you can ask them to launder what you're wearing right now. They must have guests all the time. I'm sure they'll have a spare toothbrush and toiletries, at the very least.'

'I don't want to have to ask. I don't want to be depend—' Then she remembered who she was talking to. Someone who also didn't want to be dependent on others, but who didn't have a choice because of her health.

'Darling, sometimes you have to lean on others,' Grace said, as if guessing what Tia was thinking. 'Don't worry about me. I'll be absolutely fine.'

'And you'll let me know how you are?'

'I'll text you every day while you're away,' Grace said. 'Or I'll call you. But right now you need to put yourself first.'

Something Tia had never done, and it didn't feel right for her to do that now.

As if Grace guessed, she added, 'And the baby.'

Tia thought about it.

OK. She could do this. But only for the baby's sake. And so her mother wouldn't worry.

'All right,' she said. 'But I want you to promise me you'll let me know if you need me, Mum. I mean *really* promise. Otherwise I'm going to worry myself sick about you.'

'I promise,' Grace said. 'Love you, Tia.'

'Love you, too, Mum.'

After Tia ended the call, she went in search of Antonio. He seemed to be checking something on his phone; he looked up when she walked in. 'How's your mother?'

'She's fine.' It was Tia's stock answer.

'So you'll stay here with me for a while?'

'Three days,' she said, 'until we've talked.' But she needed to make it very clear it wasn't for her own sake. 'For the baby's sake.'

'Good.' He smiled at her, and Tia was unnerved to realise that it was the first genuine smile she'd seen from him since she'd been in Casavalle. A smile that actually reached his eyes.

Antonio Valenti was absolutely gorgeous when he smiled. Tall, with melting brown eyes and dark hair that was just a shade longer than it should be for the military.

Not that she should be noticing how attractive he was, or remembering how good it had felt when he'd kissed her and touched her. They didn't have a future. All they needed to do was to talk about the baby and arrange access—if he wanted it, and she had no idea at all what he was thinking.

'And I need to let my bosses know that I'm staying here for longer than I expected,' she added. 'They'll need to arrange cover for me in my absence.'

'Of course. Call them. Then, when you're ready, we'll go to the mountains,' he said. 'My family has a house in a quiet village there— a bolt-hole, if you like. It's where I go when I need some space.'

Because, as a member of the Casavallian royal family, Antonio must live his life virtually in a goldfish bowl. He was always on public view.

'Is there any way we can stop at a shop on the way?' she asked. 'Just… I don't have anything with me. No toiletries, no pyjamas, no clean clothes.' Even if Antonio happened to have a whole wardrobe of things that his previous girlfriends or guests had left behind, it was pretty unlikely that any of them would fit a six-months-pregnant woman.

'Give me a list of everything you need and your clothing size,' he said, 'and I'll arrange things.'

He was probably used to ordering clothes from high-end designers, whereas she bought hers second-hand from charity shops. And her toiletries were supermarket own-brand basics, not from expensive Parisian perfume houses. She couldn't afford to waste money on luxuries. 'That's very kind of you,' she said carefully, 'but I'm not sure your budget would fit mine.'

He sighed. 'Look, it's my fault that you have to stay here for a few days in the first place. So please, Tia, let me buy you a few basics.'

'As long as they *are* basics,' she said. The idea of having to accept things from him made her feel awkward, even though she understood that a prince couldn't exactly go browsing in a charity shop or a supermarket. 'One change of clothes—and I assume I can have access to a washing machine and a tumble-dryer at this house in the mountains?'

'Yes. Give me a list of what you'd like,' Antonio said. 'And then we'll go to Picco Innevato.'

Snowy Peak, she translated mentally. He was taking her to a place called Snowy Peak. Well, he'd said his house was in the mountains, and it was late November. Winter. The name probably suited the place perfectly.

'OK,' she said. 'I assume we'll drive there?'

'No. We'll fly,' he said. 'I have a private jet.'

She blinked at him. 'Of course you do.' A private jet. Something far, far beyond the reach of normal mortals. She hadn't flown very often, and when she had—like today—it was always economy class. It was yet another reminder of the huge gulf between them.

'Tia, it makes sense to fly. Otherwise we'll be driving on difficult roads in the dark,' he said. 'We'll drive to the airport from here and fly over to the mountains, then drive to Picco Innevato from there. And hopefully that will mean the media won't work out where we are— or at least not until we've worked out how to manage the situation.'

Manage the situation. What a horrible way to describe a baby. OK, so she wasn't the only woman in the world who'd had an unplanned pregnancy, but right at that moment she felt more alone and miserable than she ever had before. Every nerve in her body was telling her to run back to London, where she had family and friends. What was the point of staying here to talk to Antonio? He'd made it pretty clear he wasn't interested. She was pretty sure she knew how this was going to end: with her and the baby living anonymously in London. And her baby would be very much loved; whereas here in the palace the baby would be seen as a 'situation'. If only Antonio would let her go back to London now. She'd sign any bit of paper he wanted her to, releasing him from any obligations towards herself or the baby and promising never to talk to the press. Anything. She just wanted to get out of here, be some place where she didn't feel like something people had to scrape off their shoe.

'As you wish,' she said, only just resisting the urge to add 'Your Royal Highness' and tug at her forelock, and concentrated on jotting down her list. The sooner this was over with, the better.

CHAPTER TWO

WHEN TIA HAD given Antonio her list and called her bosses to arrange an extension of her leave, Antonio's driver took them to the airport. Giacomo, one of Antonio's security officer whom she'd met in London on the evening of the charity gala, accompanied them. And it was nothing like Tia's previous experience of the airport. This time, she didn't have to wait in a queue to show her passport to the border officials, or go through any kind of security—presumably because she was travelling with a member of Casavalle's royal family. And the plane itself...

It was quite a bit smaller than the plane she'd flown on from Rome, but the interior wasn't the crammed-in rows of seats she'd experienced. This felt more like an office or a living room than an aeroplane, with deep carpeting, four massive and very comfortable-looking seats, and masses of leg room. There were tables, too, so there was plenty of room for working.

'This is how you fly all the time?' Tia asked, feeling slightly overawed by it all.

'I would normally pilot the plane myself,' Antonio said, 'but I thought you might prefer some company.'

'You can fly a plane?' She regretted the question instantly. How stupid and naive of her. Of course a man like Antonio Valenti would be able to fly a plane.

Antonio shrugged. 'I learned a few years ago.'

'And this is how you travel with your family?'

'Sort of. We don't tend to go to the same events,' he said. 'And we don't travel together. When we were young, Luca and I would travel with our nanny and our security team, not our parents.'

It hadn't occurred to her before, but now she realised that if a disaster happened in the air or on the road, it would mean the ruler and his immediate successors would all be involved. For their country's sake, of course they would have to travel separately.

'Sorry,' she mumbled.

'I'm used to it,' he said gently. 'It's how things are for me. But I realise it's not how normal families are.'

She could barely remember flying any-where with her parents and Nathan; since her father's death, either her mother hadn't been well enough to travel, or a holiday abroad had been way out of their budget. The most they'd managed in the last three or four years was the occasional day trip to Brighton, and the effort had exhausted her mother for days afterwards.

'Tell me about Picco Innevato,' she said, wanting to change the subject.

'It means "snowy peak".'

She wondered if she should tell him that she'd learned to speak Italian over the years she'd been working for Giovanni and Vittoria, but decided maybe not just yet.

'It's a very pretty village,' he said. 'In winter it serves the ski resort nearby, and in summer people go there for hiking. My family has a house on the outskirts. The villagers are good to me when I visit; they don't ask questions and they treat me as just another neighbour.'

'I guess it must be like living in a goldfish bowl when you're at the palace,' she said.

'The media are keen to know my every movement,' he admitted. 'But in Picco Innevato I can be myself. I spent quite a few summers there as a child, so I made friends with the local children. We played football and ran around in the park together.'

Things she'd taken very much for granted as a child, going to the park with her mother and Nathan and playing on the swings and slide. It had never occurred to her that other children would have a different kind of upbringing, one where they had to watch everything they did and everything they said. 'That's nice,' she said.

'It was. And I think it kept me in touch with our people better than if I'd grown up only at the palace,' he said.

For a moment, he looked sad, but she didn't want to pry. Because then he might ask her awkward questions, too—things she didn't want to answer.

'May I offer you some refreshment?' he asked. 'The flight will take about twenty minutes.'

She would've liked a cup of tea, but as the

flight was so short she could wait. 'I'm fine, thank you,' she said.

They made small talk for the rest of the journey, the kind of thing she was very good at from her job at the café, but both of them skirted round the difficult questions they'd need to discuss later. The baby. What Antonio expected from her. Whether he'd let her just go quietly back to London and disappear—which was her preferred option.

Once they'd landed, they were met by another car; this time, Antonio drove them himself, with Tia in the passenger seat next to him and Giacomo in the back of the car.

It wasn't long before they'd gone from the smooth wide roads around the airport to a narrow pass going through the mountains; the scenery was incredibly pretty, with pine trees and a dusting of snow, but the road was full of hairpin bends and there was a sharp drop straight down the mountain on one side of the car. Not wanting to distract Antonio from driving, Tia remained silent and just tried to enjoy the scenery, even though she felt as if she'd stepped into a completely different world. A magical world, like the ones her mother had read stories about when she was small—where the girl was by the side of the handsome prince and there was a happy-ever-after.

She knew it was unrealistic to expect a happy-ever-after. Her world was so different from Antonio's that she would never be able to fit in. Plus she was six months pregnant—something else you never saw in fairy tales. Of course they didn't have a future together.

Yet, out here, with the mountains and snow and fir trees all around, a tiny bit of her began to hope. Maybe they could find a way to work something out. Maybe he could be part of the baby's life. Maybe he could even be part of *her* life, too. Perhaps it was a fantasy and she'd come crashing back down to earth with a bump: but she'd definitely felt a connection with Antonio, the night they'd spent together. Something more than just sex. Something more than physical attraction. Something that made her understand the glances she'd seen between her parents as a child, that sparkle in her mother's eyes and the special smile her father had reserved for her mother. And when Antonio had kissed her, when he'd carried her to his bed, there had been something special and cherishing about his touch...

She shook herself and concentrated on her surroundings. The village of Picco Innevato was incredibly pretty. Honey-coloured stone houses with terracotta tiled roofs nestled together in the main street, and there was a church with a spire. There was a pretty square in the middle of the village with a fountain and, given that she could see people on ladders hanging Christmas lights, a space for what Tia guessed would be an amazing Christmas tree. It was a picture-postcard village—the sort she'd dreamed about when she was growing up, longing for the space of the countryside rather than being stuck in a cramped flat in a dingy part of London.

Antonio stopped at some gates at the far end of the village and tapped in a code. When the gates swung open, he drove down the long driveway and then parked in front of a large honey-coloured stone house. 'Welcome to my bolt-hole,' he said. 'Let me show you around.'

A bolt-hole to Tia meant somewhere small. This house was huge, especially in comparison with the tiny two-bedroomed flat she shared with her mother.

Feeling slightly intimidated, she followed him up the steps to the house.

Downstairs, there was a massive kitchen that was as big as their entire flat. The counter tops were all polished granite, the cupboards and drawers were solid wood and the sort she recognised from magazines as soft-closing, and the floor was terracotta tiles.

Antonio looked in the large American-style fridge and smiled. 'Excellent. Gina's stocked up for us.'

'Gina?'

'Our housekeeper,' he said. 'She lives in the village, rather than here, but I asked her to do some shopping for me.'

It made sense for Antonio's family to have someone looking after the house, as they didn't live here all the time, but Tia was finding it hard to get her head round the idea of having staff. In her world, people *were* staff. Her previous job before the café had been as a cleaner.

'I'll cook for us tonight,' he said.

Clearly he was trying to make her feel more

comfortable, and make her feel as if he was an ordinary man rather than a prince.

Except he wasn't.

He was the father of her baby.

He'd asked her to come here with him so they could talk.

And she didn't have a clue about his feelings. Or her own. The whole thing was a muddle. She couldn't afford to fall in love with someone so out of reach, even if he was the father of her baby. But, if she ignored her practical side... Being in the same room as him made her pulse skitter. It was nothing like the way she'd felt when she'd been on dates in the past. This was something that made her catch her breath, made her feel as if fireworks were going off all around her and lighting up the sky.

And she didn't know what to do about it.

Was it possible that he felt the same? This whole mixed-up yearning and wishing and wondering? Or was she just kidding herself and setting herself up for disappointment?

She forced herself to smile. 'Thank you. And I will do the washing up.'

'We'll share the washing up,' he said.

A prince, doing the washing up?

Then again, he'd told her that in the army he'd done exactly the same tasks as everyone else in his team, including cleaning. And he'd told her that this place was his bolt-hole. So maybe being a prince wasn't the lifestyle he would've chosen for himself.

He showed her around the rest of the ground floor. There was an office, a dining room with a table that seated twelve, and two large sitting rooms, both with plenty of room for several comfortable sofas and armchairs. One had a state-of-the-art television, and the other had a piano and a wall full of books. And finally there was an enormous conservatory with a view over a large and very neat garden, with the mountains looming behind.

'We're lucky here. We can see the sun setting behind the mountains in the evening, and then at sunrise, when the mountains are covered in snow, it looks all pink,' he said.

'That's lovely,' she said, but her voice must've shown that this kind of luxury and space made her feel out of place.

'Tia,' he said gently, 'it's all relative. I know this is a bit big for a normal person's bolt-hole, but please remember it isn't just my house. It belongs to my family. And our security team needs a bedroom and a bathroom each, plus sometimes we have guests to stay.'

'Uh-huh,' she said.

Upstairs, there were eight enormous bedrooms, all with their own bathrooms.

'I thought you might like this room, because it has a view over the mountains,' he said, showing her to one bedroom. It was a fairytale suite; the king-sized brass bedstead had deep pillows, a thick duvet and pretty floral bedlinen. The beautifully carved dressing table had an ornate mirror; to one side of the room there were doors that she assumed opened to a built-in wardrobe. There was a comfortable armchair by the window; the small coffee table next to it had a vase of beautiful pink and white roses and copies of the latest glossy women's magazines—in English, she noted, so had they been bought with her in mind?

The bathroom was huge, too: a marble floor and marble walls, a deep bathtub, a shower cubicle with an enormous shower head and what looked like jets coming out of the walls, a gilt mirror above the sink, and a shelf that was already stocked with toiletries and a new toothbrush still in its packaging. She recognised the brands as ones that she couldn't even afford as special presents when they were discounted in the post-Christmas sales. This was sheer unadulterated luxury, and a whole world away from her normal life.

'I hope these are OK,' he said, gesturing to the shelf.

'I... Thank you.' She'd work out later how to replace the toiletries for him. It would put quite a hole in her budget, but she'd always been good at juggling.

'Gina bought a couple of changes of clothes for you,' he said, 'and she put them away in the wardrobe and the dressing table. Though if you'd prefer a different room, I can move everything for you.'

He'd managed to arrange clothes for her already? She stared at him in surprise. 'But I only gave you that list an hour ago!'

He shrugged. 'Picco Innevato might look small, but there are a few shops here. As I said, the village is used as a ski resort in winter, and people come for the hiking in the summer.'

If it was a touristy place, then the clothes sold here would be by expensive designer boutiques rather than cheap and cheerful chain stores or supermarkets, she thought.

As if he was guessing what she was thinking, he said gently, 'It's my fault that you're here as my guest, so I'm simply providing you with a couple of changes of clothes, just as any of my family would do for a guest staying here. The same goes for the toiletries. There are no strings, Tia, and I'll be very offended if you offer to pay for them.'

Although Tia wanted to argue and tell him that she could manage to buy her own clothes, thank you very much, she had the baby to think about—and the fact that she'd be on maternity leave in a couple of months, reducing her budget even further. Which meant she'd have to swallow her pride and accept his kindness. 'Thank you,' she said, feeling miserable and selfish and totally mixed up. She had never relied on anyone in her life, and she didn't want to start now. But, for the sake of the baby and her mother, she might have to.

It would help if she had a better idea of what *he* wanted. The man, not the Prince. But how could she ask without sounding ungrateful? She was stuck.

'Take your time settling in,' he said. 'If you want to take a bath or shower to freshen up, or have a nap, that's fine. We're not on palace time. And call your mother to let her know you're here safely. I'll be downstairs when you're ready.'

'Thank you.'

He left her to look over the clothes. And they were utterly gorgeous—a couple of long-sleeved silky maternity tops, a pair of maternity trousers, a soft cashmere cardigan, a smart black skirt and a pretty floral tunic dress. There was underwear, too, and maternity tights. Three pairs of pyjamas, with soft jersey trousers and lace-trimmed matching camisole tops.

Tia's eyes filled with tears. They were so pretty. And this was so kind of his housekeeper, to do this for a complete stranger.

Antonio made himself a coffee, but he didn't feel as relaxed as he usually did here in his bolt-hole.

What was he going to do about Tia Phillips?

He saw her through a haze of guilt: his best friend's little sister. The woman he should've supported after her brother's death, but he'd let her down. The woman he'd let comfort him. The woman he'd made pregnant—albeit unknowingly—and abandoned.

The woman, if he was honest with himself, who made him feel different—as if he was more than just the younger Prince of Casavalle or a team commander. She made him feel as if she saw right through the pomp and the public face to the man behind it. Just like that night they'd spent together, when she'd comforted him and let him comfort her: he had no idea why, but she'd broken through all his barriers. Though he didn't want to examine it too closely and work out why she was the only one who'd made him feel that way. Emotional stuff made him antsy because he'd never really learned how to deal with it—and he didn't want to deal with it now. Duty was much, much easier than emotion.

Just put it down to sexual attraction, he told himself, and move on.

Because his duty to Casavalle had to come first. He had to think about the baby and what it would mean for his country. And then he would do the right thing.

Miles would be discreet, Antonio knew. So

he had a breathing space before he had to tell his family the truth about the 'personal matters to attend to' he'd texted them about. And he had absolutely no idea how they would react to the news of the baby. His mother would be furious. His brother—although Luca knew that Tia had tried to contact Antonio, he didn't know why, so he would be shocked. Gabriella... She was an 'unexpected' baby herself, so she might have a different viewpoint.

But he knew they'd all be disappointed in him.

What he'd done had been very far from hon-ourable, even though it was completely unin-tentional. And he needed to fix the situation. Now.

He'd never thought he'd settle down and have children. When they'd been growing up, it was always assumed that Luca—as the el-dest son—would take over from their father, and Luca would be the one who had to marry someone suitable and produce the next heir to the throne. The arrangement with Princess Meribel had happened years ago, so Antonio had had the freedom to join the army, travel-ling the world and taking on dangerous missions. He'd loved every second of his job and he'd relished his freedom. He'd been planning to go back to the army once Luca was settled as the King of Casavalle—or Gabriella as the new Queen. Either way, his time in Casavalle had been temporary.

Now… Now it was different. He was going to be a father. Going back to the army and putting himself in danger was less of an option now. He had responsibilities: emotional as well as financial.

And that was the problem.

Emotional stuff. The thing he found difficult.

Growing up, he remembered both of his parents being very formal and his father had been distant. Antonio couldn't remember his father ever hugging him, or saying he loved his younger son, or saying that he was proud of him. He'd worked hard in the army and he'd earned his promotions through merit, not through his connections; but King Vincenzo had never acknowledged that or made any comment about how hard his son had worked. Queen Maria was warmer but, like his father, she'd always encouraged him to put his civic duty before his feelings.

And, although Antonio had dated plenty of women, he'd never felt a real connection with any of them. He'd enjoyed their company, but had always made it clear right from the start that the relationship was strictly short term.

Except for Tia, a little voice said in his head.

Tia Phillips, with her soft brown eyes, her tumble of black curls, and her petite frame that hid amazing inner strength. When he had seen her again today in the palace, he'd felt that leap of his pulse, the slow burn of pleasure that was more intense than he'd ever experienced with anyone else. If he was honest with himself, she was the only person he'd ever really felt connected to. That night in London when they'd shared their grief over losing her brother and held each other tightly. That night when she'd broken through all his barriers. The night when they'd made a baby...

The baby.

Antonio took the photograph she'd given him from his wallet. The baby was lying on his back, knees up, and one arm was raised so Antonio could see a tiny hand. Fingers.

Their baby.

He dragged in a breath. It was miraculous and terrifying at the same time.

And Tia had been dealing with this alone.

The more he thought about it, the more he knew he had to do the right thing by her. Marry her, make their child legitimate, support her. And she'd looked so worried when she'd sat in the palace secretary's office, waiting to tell him the news. Guilt squeezed his insides again as he thought about it. Did she really think he'd abandon her for a third time?

Then again, he hadn't given her any reason to think he'd do anything else. He'd abandoned her and her mother after breaking the news of Nathan's death, and he hadn't got in touch again after the charity gala. Where Tia was concerned, he had a really terrible track record.

So when she came downstairs, he'd reassure her. Tell her they would get married.

On the other hand, he knew that Tia was an independent woman. Extremely independent, according to Nathan; she'd spent her life being their mother's carer, putting her own dreams aside. Dreams of travelling the world and becoming a primary school teacher, so Nathan had said.

In that case, would she even agree to marry him, even though it was the right thing for the baby?

But Antonio knew it was the right thing to do. If they got married, he could fulfil his duties as the baby's father, and he could help Tia with her mother. He could bring Grace Phillips over to Casavalle, where the climate might be better for her health and she'd have access to much more support than she had in London. Then Tia would be able to be Grace's daughter rather than her carer; and, although Tia would need to support him in his royal duties so she wouldn't have the time to become a primary school teacher, she would at least be able to travel the world with him.

And maybe Luca—or Gabriella, whichever of them was crowned—would allow him to have some kind of special responsibilities for education, so Tia could fulfil her dreams that way, working with him.

He had the whole thing sorted perfectly in his head by the time Tia came downstairs.

'Is everything all right? Is there anything you need?' he asked.

'Thank you, everything's lovely. I'm fine.'

He noticed there was a slight disconnect between her words and her expression; although she was smiling, it didn't reach her eyes. He wasn't quite sure what was wrong, but she definitely wasn't fine. 'Tea?' he asked.

'No, thank you.'

Or maybe she was worrying about his reaction to the baby. Maybe she needed reassurance. He could sort that out right now.

'Let's go into the conservatory,' he said.

Giacomo had tactfully gone to his own room, giving Antonio and Tia the space they needed to talk.

Tia let the Prince usher her through to the conservatory and settle her on one of the comfortable sofas.

'I've been thinking,' he said. 'There's a very simple solution to this. We'll get married.'

Married?

Just like that?

Tia stared at him in disbelief.

Of course Prince Antonio didn't want to marry her. He didn't love her. He clearly didn't feel anything towards her except a sense of duty and honour. He hadn't hugged her, he hadn't told her he'd missed her—in fact, he'd barely even touched her other than to support her elbow as she'd climbed the steps to the plane, which she was fairly sure he'd do for any female he accompanied because it was a very regal and very polite thing to do. And, even though her skin had tingled when his hand had accidentally brushed against hers, she was pretty sure it hadn't been the same for him.

Prince Antonio of the House of Valenti was an unemotional *machine*.

Yes, he could put people at their ease— because that was what royals were trained to do. It was all about duty, where he was concerned. He hadn't brought her here to his bolt-hole because he wanted to spend time with her, but because he needed to get her away from the media and protect his family's privacy.

His suggestion of marriage was utterly ridiculous. She hadn't come here to demand he do the old-fashioned 'right thing' by her; her sole intention had been to let him know about the baby's existence and then leave. She'd managed the six months of her pregnancy so far perfectly well without him, and she'd manage the birth and their child's life in exactly the same way.

She'd been born to a couple who hadn't been married but who had loved each other deeply and who'd adored their children. OK, so maybe it had turned out that her dad was wrong about marriage being just a bit of paper; but she understood where he was coming from. You should be with someone because you loved them and the world felt like a better place because they were in it, not because you were bound by a contract.

No way was Tia getting married to a man who didn't want her and who saw their baby as a burden and a duty. That was the complete opposite of what her parents had had. It wasn't what she wanted. At all. Yes, it was honourable of him to suggest the marriage, and she appreciated that: but marriage would be completely the wrong thing for both of them.

'No,' she said.

Antonio looked taken aback.

Which wasn't so surprising: she very much doubted he'd ever heard the word 'no' when he was growing up. Everyone around him was more likely to have said, 'Yes, Your Royal Highness,' bowed deeply and done exactly what the little imperious Prince had demanded.

'No?' he asked, clearly expecting her to say she'd made a mistake and of course she would marry him.

'No,' she said.

'Why?'

Because you're an automaton who has no real emotions.

Not that it would be tactful to say so. But she could still tell him the rest of the truth.

'Because,' she said, 'you don't love me. You're asking me to marry you because of the baby. Because you think it's the honourable thing to do.' Hadn't he talked about honour before, about not letting Princess Meribel take the blame for her own actions even though she'd been the one to behave badly? 'That isn't what I want. So I'm not going to marry you.'

He blew out a breath. 'Tia, this baby is fourth in line to the throne.'

'Not if I don't marry you, he isn't.'

Antonio's eyes widened. 'The baby's definitely a boy?'

'I don't know. They can't always tell on a scan, and I chose not to find out. But I don't want to call the baby "it"; he's a person, not a thing.'

'Fair enough.' Antonio looked at her. 'But I don't understand how you can say that my child isn't in line to the throne.'

'Because surely any heir to the throne has to be legitimate?' she asked. 'Which means we have a very obvious solution to the problem. If you don't marry me, then the baby isn't legitimate and therefore won't be your heir—and that means you have no legal obligations to either of us.'

'It's a matter of honour,' he said stiffly.

Just what she'd thought. This was all about honour, not love. 'My parents loved each other deeply,' she said quietly, 'and I'm not settling for anything less than that. My answer's still no. I won't marry you.'

He frowned. 'Tia, I know I've let you down twice now, and I apologise deeply for that. But I won't make that mistake a third time.'

No, he wouldn't—because she wasn't giving him the chance to do that. She spread her hands. 'I'm not making any demands on you whatsoever. I've already explained to you that I told you about the baby purely out of courtesy. Because I thought you ought to know. Not because I expected anything from you. Marriage isn't an option.'

He raked a hand through his hair, and the slight disarray made him look more human. Touchable. Not the cold, emotionless Prince who'd greeted her at the palace, but Antonio the man.

Oh, help. She needed to get a grip.

Touching really wasn't what she should be thinking about right now.

Touching was what had got her into this situation in the first place. Holding him, because she'd felt sorry for him and thought that a hug would comfort both of them. Except hugging had turned to kissing, which had turned to him carrying her to his bed, which had turned out to be the most amazing night of her life...

Antonio Valenti wasn't the only man she'd slept with, but he was the only one she'd felt a real connection to. He'd made her feel different. Special, as if she was really important to him. The differences between their social positions hadn't mattered; it had been just the two of them, and that night she'd felt as if the Prince had seen her for who she really was, not just the cheerful waitress with a complicated home life.

She'd responded to him on a deeper level than she had to anyone else before; it was a fact that scared her and thrilled her in equal measure. She didn't want to be emotionally dependent on a man who kept his emotions in check all the time. She definitely didn't want to fall in love with someone who couldn't love her back.

But between them that night they'd managed to make a baby.

Now she was facing the consequences.

What should she do now?

Antonio was gorgeous. A total fairy-tale prince, except he was real. And that weird feeling she got when she looked at him—it wasn't the baby kicking. It felt more as if her heart was doing some kind of weird somersault, something that wasn't even anatomically possible.

But how could he ever be really hers? He had responsibilities towards his country, so if he ever settled down with someone it'd have to be for dynastic reasons. His wife would probably have to be at least the daughter of a duke, if not an actual princess.

Which meant there was no real future in any relationship between Antonio and herself, despite the baby and his offer of marriage just now. He probably shouldn't even have asked her to marry him without checking with the palace first. If she let herself act on the pull she felt towards him, she'd just be making a fool of herself, and it wouldn't help either of them. She needed to be cool-headed and calm. And utterly, utterly sensible. He didn't love her. And her own feelings towards him were so muddled that she couldn't make sense of them.

'I am *not* marrying you,' she repeated.

Antonio really hadn't expected this.

Tia had refused his proposal of marriage because she wanted to get married for love?

But that was something that just didn't happen in his family. King Vincenzo had learned the hard way from his first marriage, to Sophia Ross. He'd married for love, and look how that had turned out. Sophia hadn't been able to cope with a royal lifestyle. She'd left Vincenzo to go back home to Canada; she hadn't told him that she was expecting a baby, and Gabriella had grown up completely unaware of who she really was.

Then it occurred to him that Tia at least

hadn't done what Sophia had done. She hadn't kept the baby secret.

He thought about it some more. His parents' own marriage had been arranged and it had been successful; his father had grown to love his mother, even though he hadn't shown any affection outwardly. But the arranged marriage between his older brother and Princess Meribel had gone badly wrong, because Meribel had been rash and chasing after true love instead of being sensible and joining their two countries' dynasties. Arranged marriages meant that you had to make compromises, but that went with the territory of being a royal. You had to put your country's needs before your own desires. Luca and Imogen had fallen in love and got engaged; maybe his elder brother was just lucky, Antonio thought. Because, on the whole, his own family's experience had taught him that relationships based on love tended to end up in a mess.

Why couldn't Tia see that you couldn't rely on love? That honour and duty was a better solution?

His head was spinning.

Right now he didn't know what to think. He

was filled with guilt for the way he'd treated Tia; he was still trying to get his head round the changes in his own family; he missed his best friend and he missed his father, at the same time as he wished that things had maybe been different and he'd been able to make Vincenzo as proud of him as of his elder brother Luca.

And now there was the baby to think about. He was still trying to process the fact that he was going to be a father. Duty said the right thing to do would be to marry Tia and give the baby his name. But there was more to being a parent than just creating a baby. Would he be any good at it? Would he be able to give his child more than his parents had given him— the kind of warmth his best friend had exuded when he'd talked about his parents? Was Tia right and she'd be better off as a single mum, without him bumbling around and making a mess of things because he didn't really know how to do emotional stuff?

He couldn't find the right words to say to her.

And clearly she wasn't impressed by his silence, because she added, 'And that's an end to the matter.'

Oh, no, it wasn't.

They needed to talk about this properly and work things through. Together.

Tia was having *his* baby. And he could give her and the baby the security they needed. His best friend would never be able to follow his dreams, thanks to the land mine that had blown up his armoured car; but perhaps Antonio could give Tia the chance to follow her dreams.

He just had to persuade her to give him a chance, too.

'Tia—'

'It's not up for discussion,' she said. 'We are *not* getting married.'

Nathan had been proud of his little sister's independence, but right now Antonio was starting to get a bit annoyed by her stubbornness. He wanted her to help him here. Be reasonable.

But he realised that demanding that she marry him wasn't going to convince her that marriage was the right thing to do. He needed to persuade her. Turn on a charm offensive, maybe. He needed to take the emotion out of it, the way he always did. Make it a military operation and treat it as clear-headedly as he treated his work: Operation Persuade Tia.

So for now he'd make a tactical retreat. 'OK.'

She looked slightly shocked, as if she hadn't expected him to agree so quickly. So what did she want? Had she wanted him to fight for her affections?

Love and affection wasn't something he'd thought to have. He wasn't entirely sure that he wanted them; he'd seen what a mess they could cause. Yet, on the other hand, he knew there was something missing from his life. Something he rather thought might be important. All the short-term relationships with no promises, no future: if he was honest with himself, they'd stopped being fun a long time ago. But he'd never met anyone who'd made him think that there could be something more. Not until Tia.

'But,' he said, 'we do need to talk.'

'About what?'

'Everything we didn't say at the palace. But now we've got the space and time to talk properly. Let me make that cup of tea, first,' he prevaricated. The English solution to everything, he thought wryly.

At least she didn't argue about *that*.

He left her in the conservatory, swiftly busied himself in the kitchen, and made two mugs of tea.

'Thank you,' she said when he returned and handed her a mug.

'So when did you realise that you were pregnant?' he asked.

'A couple of months after—' She stopped, and blushed.

After they'd comforted each other and it had turned into lovemaking. Yeah. He didn't want to say that out loud, either. He didn't want to unpick the feelings he'd ignored since then.

'I was busy, I lost track of the time, and it didn't occur to me that my period was late.' She sipped her tea and looked away. 'When I finally realised that my period was late, I did a test.' She paused. 'I probably should've tried to tell you about it back then.'

Why hadn't she?

Clearly she anticipated his question—that, or it was written all over his face—because she continued, 'It took me a while to come to terms with being pregnant and think about what I wanted. Especially when—' She stopped.

'When what?'

'You're photographed with a *lot* of women. The celeb magazines talk about you and your dates all the time. They say that you're a playboy.'

Which wasn't what she wanted from her baby's father? He could understand that. And it wasn't who he was. He grimaced. 'I don't sleep with every woman I date. And I have to show my face at a lot of events where I'm expected to bring a plus one. The media try to spin stories when there isn't really anything to say. I'm not a playboy.'

He hadn't been in a relationship with Tia; but maybe he hadn't been as honest with her as he had been with his usual dates. And even though he hadn't been dating Tia so technically he hadn't cheated on her, he'd been out with other women while Tia was pregnant with his baby—which felt like cheating. Even though he hadn't known about the baby at the time. And it made him feel really, really guilty.

Uncomfortable with the direction his thoughts were taking, he turned the subject back to the baby. 'And you want to keep the baby.'

She nodded. 'What happened… It's not the baby's fault.'

'No.' And it hadn't even occurred to Antonio that there might be consequences from that night. He hadn't thought of anything at all recently except his family's situation. They were all still getting used to the new order of things, following his father's death. Trying to support their people and their country, not letting their personal feelings show. He'd kept busy, but inside he'd felt lost and empty, missing his father and missing his best friend, unable to talk to anyone about how he felt.

The only person he'd come close to confiding in was Tia, the night of the charity gala, when they'd turned to each other for comfort. Having her here, close to him again, made him antsy. Part of him wanted that closeness back; yet, at the same time, that closeness had led them to this tricky situation.

Right now, he thought grimly, he could do with the equivalent of an armoured car so he could lock his heart safely away in it.

So what were they going to do?

He'd used a condom when he'd made love with Tia, but clearly the protection had failed. Or maybe it had happened the second time they'd made love, when they'd both been half-asleep and seeking comfort from each other. He wasn't entirely sure he'd used a condom then so, actually, this whole thing was his fault. He should've been the one who'd been responsible. He should've kept himself under control.

'I'm sorry,' he said.

'It is as it is,' she said with a shrug. 'Mum and I manage. And my bosses have been great. Vittoria, my boss, fusses over me a bit and makes sure I sit down between the really busy periods.'

Then it occurred to him what her job was. She was a waitress in a coffee shop. Which meant that she'd be on her feet all the time, taking orders, ferrying drinks and snacks to the customers, clearing tables and rushing about—because, from what Antonio had learned from her brother, Tia Phillips wasn't the sort to slack off and expect other people to shoulder her duties. 'Is that good for you and the baby, being on your feet all day?' he asked.

Within seconds he knew he'd asked the wrong question. She had that stubborn, independent set to her jaw he was beginning to realise meant trouble. 'Women have managed to stay on their feet and work while they're pregnant for hundreds of years, Antonio.'

'Yes. Of course. I apologise.'

Though at least she'd used his given name, rather than calling him 'Your Royal Highness' or awkwardly not calling him anything at all. Funny how that made him feel warm inside; and it made him feel wrong-footed at the same time.

He wasn't used to women making him feel in a spin.

What was it about Tia Phillips that was so different? And how could he get everything back under his control, the way it usually was?

'I eat properly and I rest properly, before you ask,' she said.

He didn't quite believe her on the 'resting' bit. He knew that she was still caring for her mother, meaning that she must be doing the majority of looking after the house and preparing meals when her mother wasn't well, plus she was handling the demands of her job.

'And, as soon as I realised I was pregnant, I started taking folic acid. I know it was a bit late, but it was better than nothing. Mum makes sure I take a vitamin tablet for pregnant women every morning,' she said.

'That's good,' he said, not knowing what else to say.

He was good in social situations. He'd been good at leading his team in the army, he'd been diplomatic with Meribel's family, and he'd helped Gabriella to feel more at ease in the palace, knowing from his experiences in the army how overwhelming the life of a royal could seem to someone who hadn't been brought up in it.

But with Tia, right now, he was all at sixes and sevens. She wasn't reacting the way he expected her to react. Plus, if he was honest with himself, she made him feel things he'd never felt before. A kind of yearning, mixed with something he couldn't quite put his finger on. Not nervousness, exactly, and not the adrenalin rush he was used to at work. This was deeper, tangled up with his emotions, so he couldn't compartmentalise it, and it unsettled him.

'You've had regular appointments with the hospital?' he asked, trying to bring things back to facts. Unemotional facts that he could deal with.

'Only the dating scan and the twenty-week

scan—the one where they gave me the photograph. The rest of my appointments are with the community midwife. And, yes, I've gone to every single one.'

There was a slight edge to her tone. 'I wasn't accusing you of putting the baby at risk,' he said quietly. 'I'm concerned about *you*.'

Colour flared into her face. 'Sorry. I didn't mean to snap. I guess...' She grimaced. 'Blame it on the hormones?'

The situation couldn't be easy for her, either. He inclined his head. 'Of course. So your plan after telling me the news was to go back home, have the baby, and then someone would look after the baby while you work?'

'I have a friend who's expecting a baby and she's also a waitress,' Tia explained. 'We were going to try to work out some kind of arrangement, so while one of us was working the other would look after both the babies. That way neither of us would have to pay for childcare, and we'd both be able to spend time with our babies. Although I don't know how realistic that would be.'

But doing that would also mean that Tia would be working fewer hours, which in turn meant she'd be earning less than she did now. Money would be really, really tight. Especially as Nathan was no longer able to help out financially.

Antonio had to find a way around her pride.

And the best way to do that was to persuade her to marry him.

If she insisted on marrying for love… Then somehow he had to make her fall in love with him, and make her believe that he'd fallen in love with her. And then finally she'd let him help her.

'I can see you've thought everything through,' he said.

She narrowed her eyes at him. 'Are you being sarcastic with me?'

'No. Actually, I think your ability to work out a strategy to manage any situation is every bit as good as any general I've worked with,' he said.

She went slightly pink. 'Oh. Thank you.'

'And I appreciate you coming here with me. I didn't bring you here because I'm ashamed of you—or of what we did.'

Her blush deepened. 'Uh-huh.'

Interesting. So maybe she wasn't completely immune to him.

He wasn't immune to her, either.

Not that he was going to let his emotions cloud things. Emotions just made things messy. If the idea of love made it easier for her to accept his proposal of marriage, then fair enough. But he was keeping his mind clear. He wasn't letting his heart rule his head.

'I brought you here,' he continued, 'because I wanted us to have the space to talk, without any pressure. Because what *you* want is important.' And hopefully he could persuade her to want what he wanted, too.

'So you're not going to railroad me into anything?'

'No.' He was going to charm her into doing what he felt was best for them all. And there was a difference. He wasn't a bully. He wanted to look after her and the baby properly, and he wanted her to accept his help willingly. 'These three days are all about us getting to know each other a bit better. Understanding each other.'

'That works for me,' she said. 'Thank you.'

'So perhaps you'll agree to have dinner with me this evening,' he said. 'I'll cook.'

She frowned. 'I don't expect you to wait on me.'

'I thought that maybe we could prepare dinner together,' he said. Doing things together might help. Working as a team. It might show her that they could be good together, despite being near-strangers.

And then she might agree to marry him—and all the fuss and confusion could stop.

CHAPTER THREE

TOGETHER, THEY WATCHED the sun set over the mountains, the sky striped in shades of pink and blue and gold against the snow-capped peaks.

'It's beautiful here,' Tia said. 'I can see why you come here when you need a bolt-hole. But you said the media follows you everywhere. Does that mean they follow you here?'

'Not as much as they'd like to,' Antonio said. 'The villagers are fairly protective of me, probably because they remember me coming here as a child and some of them remember playing with Luca and me when we were young. They're fairly good at misdirection when it comes to the media. And I'm very grateful for it.'

'It must be hard, having to be in the public eye so much.'

'It's one of the reasons why I appreciate being in the army,' he said. 'Obviously the media don't cover me at work, because they know that would be putting me and my team at risk. But, yes, one's position as a royal can be tricky. It's the way things are so easily misinterpreted, the way people look for hidden meanings that just aren't there.' He shrugged. 'But it is what it is. Shall we go and find something for dinner?'

'That'd be nice,' she said.

He ushered her into the kitchen.

'So what do you like to eat?' he asked.

'I eat practically anything. I'm not fussy.'

He coughed. 'Even *I* know that there are things women need to avoid eating in pregnancy, and things that they need to eat for the baby's sake.'

'I'm just going into the third trimester,' she said, 'so I need lots of calcium.'

'So that's milk and cheese, right?'

'As long as it's pasteurised. And lots of dark green leafy veg, dried apricots, sardines and that sort of thing.' She grimaced. 'Though not too much spice, please, as I've discovered that garlic and very spicy foods give me heartburn.'

He looked through the vegetable drawers in the fridge. 'We have spinach and kale, and Gina's bought chicken, but I'll get some sardines ordered in for tomorrow, if you like.' He looked in the cupboards. 'We have dried apricots and couscous, so I could make you a sort of chicken tagine, with spinach and kale stirred in, and I'll keep the spices mild.'

She was surprised. 'You can actually cook a tagine?'

'I learned while I was in the army. With a team assembled from many different countries, you get to learn about other people's cultures and ideas. Thanks to that, I've learned quite a bit about food, and making stews over a fire. And in return I taught my team how to make a really good tomato sauce for pasta, and how not to over-cook pasta.' He rolled his eyes. 'My team-mates only ever served me soggy spaghetti once. And don't get me started on pasta in a tin with that orange stuff claiming to be *sauce.*'

This was a side of him she hadn't really seen. She could understand now why her brother had been friends with him: there was a slight bite to his humour. This side of Prince Antonio, the more human side that he clearly didn't let show very often, was one she rather liked. A man whose company she could enjoy—much more than the formal, slightly stuffy royal personage who bossed her about and irritated her.

'You miss the army, don't you?' she asked.

'I do,' he admitted. 'Yes, there are days when I see terrible things that no human should ever have to see, but it's a job where my team and I can make a real difference. Where we can help people.'

'Will you go back to it?'

'If my father had still been alive, I would've been back with my team now,' he said. 'But at the moment my brother, my mother and my new sister need me.'

She could understand that—and she liked the fact that family was important to him.

'So can you take a sabbatical until things settle down, or will you have to leave the army?'

'I'm on special leave for now, but I'll do what it takes to support my family and my country.'

She wasn't entirely sure whether that meant he put his duty first or his family first. Or maybe they were one and the same for someone in a royal family. 'So you'd be happy to stay at the palace?'

He looked at her, as if weighing it up. 'This stays between you and me?'

'Of course,' she said. 'I have no intention of running to the media and gossiping.'

'I was thinking less of the media and more of my family,' he said dryly. 'But OK. Thank you. The palace I can handle. But the politics drives me insane.' He rolled his eyes. 'The senseless squabbles and point-scoring between people. I want to bang their heads together and tell them to stop behaving like pompous kindergarteners boasting "My dad's more important than yours" because there are so many more important problems in the world that need solving, and you solve things much more effectively if you work together as a team.'

She grinned. 'I guess you'd get into a lot of trouble if you did that.'

'Yes. I don't know how my brother copes with it.' He wrinkled his nose. 'Well, I do. He was brought up knowing that he'd serve our country. He's trained for the job.'

'What about your half-sister?' The woman who might end up being Queen.

'She didn't even know who she was until this year,' Antonio said. 'Her mother, Sophia, never told her about her heritage—and Sophia died when Gabriella was three, so Gabriella was brought up by her aunt and uncle. She ran a bookshop in Canada. She certainly wasn't brought up the way Luca and I were. And then she found a letter from her mother while she was clearing out. She contacted my mother to find out the truth of it—and obviously as she's older than Luca that would make her my father's heir. The DNA test will prove things beyond doubt.'

'Do you think she's your father's daughter?'

'Yes. I look at her and I can see my father,' Antonio said. 'A softer, warmer version.'

So his childhood hadn't been idyllic? If his father had been formal and cold, it would explain why Antonio suppressed his emotions. Why he didn't seem to believe in love.

'Is she nice?'

'I like her,' Antonio said. 'She's sensible. I think she's a lot like Luca.'

'It must be hard, suddenly discovering you're not who you think you are,' Tia said. 'And having to do it in the public eye.'

'She's strong. She'll cope. Plus,' Antonio added, 'there is the palace library. Hundreds and hundreds of rare volumes. I think that will

be her bolt-hole. A place where she'll be surrounded by books.'

Antonio's bolt-hole meant that he was surrounded by mountains. Was he trying to tell
her something? Or was she reading too much
into it?

He let her prepare the vegetables and the couscous while he sizzled the chicken and made the
sauce for the stew, and soon the kitchen was
filled with a delicious scent.

'I'll just go and see if Giacomo wants to eat
with us,' Antonio said. 'I'll be back in a minute or two.'

Tia sat down and sipped a glass of water, re-
flecting on what she'd learned about Antonio.
It sounded as if his childhood had been lonely;
although his family was wealthy, it didn't seem
as if he had the same close bond that she and
Nathan had had with their parents before their
father died. And because everything was so
formal at the palace, it would explain why he'd
seemed so reserved and emotionless there.

Maybe he wasn't really like that, inside. And
hadn't he said something about the media making up a story when there was nothing to tell?
Maybe he'd grown up not trusting himself to

show any feelings, in case they were misreported and it made waves for his family.

Poor little rich boy.

If she'd had to choose between her own impoverished childhood filled with love and his wealthy childhood filled with rules and regulations, it would've been an easy choice. She'd pick love, all the way.

Could Antonio learn to love? Could he be a real father to their baby and a partner to her? Could they actually make this work?

Or would it be kinder to all of them if she just disappeared quietly back to London?

Antonio came back into the kitchen. 'Giacomo says he's going to have something later, in his room.'

'Does that mean he's speaking from experience and he knows your cooking doesn't taste as good as it smells?' she asked.

Instead of looking slightly affronted, he surprised her by laughing. 'No. But he's probably going to taste this, pull a face and add a lot of garlic and chilli.'

And now she felt guilty. She'd been the one to ask him not to use garlic or spices. Antonio, too, would probably find the meal tasteless. She could put up with the indigestion. All she'd have to do was sit upright for most of the night and take frequent sips of water. 'Sorry. Please don't think about what I said. Add the garlic and chi—'

'It's fine, Tia,' he cut in. 'I'm happy to eat the same as you. Shall we eat in the dining room?'

'Could we eat here in the kitchen?' she asked. 'Otherwise the two of us are going to be a bit lost, sitting at a table big enough for twelve.'

'Sure.'

She laid the table while Antonio dished up. And he was surprised by how nice it felt, eating in the kitchen with her: how cosy and domestic. It was a world he'd never really experienced. It had never occurred to him before that this existed: this feeling of being settled, of belonging, of being close to someone.

Home.

He'd never yearned for domesticity before. He'd enjoyed travelling the world and the adrenalin rush of his job, knowing that he was making a difference. But settling down… Now he was beginning to see what it could be like.

And he was shocked to discover how much he wanted this.

'This is good,' she said when she tasted the tagine.

'Not too garlicky or spicy?' he checked.

'It's perfect,' she said. 'Thank you for accommodating me.'

'My pleasure.' Though he was uneasy about behaving like polite strangers to each other when they'd been so much more than that. Her very obvious baby bump was proof of what they'd been to each other, for that one night. And, even though it made him antsy thinking about the way she'd made him feel, at the same time he wanted that closeness back. Here, in the one place he could remember having fun as a child and where he felt free of the restrictions of the palace, he wanted to keep her talking to him. Maybe starting with a neutral topic would help. 'So what do you think of Casavalle?'

'The village here and the mountains are beautiful. And your palace is a bit like a fairy-tale castle, all pure white stone and turrets,' she said.

He'd never really thought about it like that before. 'I suppose so.'

'And that Christmas tree in the palace foyer is amazing,' she said. 'It must've taken ages to decorate.'

'We have a team in charge of decorating the palace,' he said.

She smiled. 'I guess you can't have the King of Casavalle climbing up a ladder and reaching across the branches.'

'We use scaffolding for a tree of that height, actually, but you're right.' He looked at her, suddenly curious. She'd focused on the tree. Christmas for him was a time of duty, but had it been different for her? 'What were Christmases like when you were young?'

'We'd put the tree up as soon as Dad came home on leave, the week before Christmas,' she said. 'We'd go and choose one together, as a family—a real one that smelled lovely. And then Dad would put the lights on, and Mum would get out the box of decorations and we'd all take turns in putting an ornament on the tree. Each year Nathan and I would choose a new one in the shop, and we'd have one each that we'd made at nursery or school.' She smiled. 'Yogurt pots we'd painted and covered in glitter and decorated with a tinsel loop so they looked like a bell, or a star we'd cut out and glued pasta on and spray-painted gold, and an angel made out of a cardboard tube, a ping-pong ball, scraps of fabric and wool. Mum kept every single one of the ones we made; even though they're too worn to go on the tree nowadays, she can't bear to throw them away.'

A small family Christmas, with decorations on the tree that had meaning and had been made with love, rather than being bought *en masse* from a retailer, or priceless baubles that had been part of the family for decades but were never allowed to be played with. So very different from his own. What would it have been like to grow up in a warm, close family like that?

'And every year on Christmas Eve we'd hang our stockings at the foot of the bed. Mum made them herself—she's amazing with a needle—and she embroidered our names and stars on them with silver thread so they sparkled. We'd set out a glass of milk and a chocolate biscuit for Father Christmas, and a carrot for his reindeer; and every year we'd come down to find an empty glass, a plate with just crumbs on it, and a half-eaten carrot.'

His family had never had traditions like that. He couldn't even remember when he'd stopped believing in Father Christmas.

'When we were little, our stockings would be filled with sweets and a couple of tangerines, a colouring book and crayons, maybe a toy car for Nathan and a bottle of bubbles with a wand for me.' She smiled. 'Even after Dad died and money was a bit tight, Mum would still fill a stocking for us. She used to buy a little something every couple of weeks and she'd hide the gifts away in a box at the top of her wardrobe so we wouldn't find them. On Christmas Eve, we'd go to midnight mass with Mum in the church round the corner and sing carols, then come home to have hot chocolate and marshmallows before going to bed.

'Even when we stopped believing in Father Christmas, we still put our stockings out. Nathan and I used to make a stocking for Mum, too. We'd save our pocket money and buy her nice bath stuff from the market and make her photo frames, that sort of thing. She cried the first year we did it, and we were so worried we'd upset her, but she told us how special the stocking was and how much she loved us.'

Love. A word that was never really used in the palace. Their father had always been distant, even here; although their mother was warmer, Queen Maria was very practical and didn't tend to talk about emotional things. And, although Antonio loved his brother and looked up to him, he wasn't sure he'd ever actually told Luca he loved him, and Luca certainly hadn't said it to him. They just didn't do that sort of thing.

And now he was beginning to wonder if he'd missed out. If his childhood had been so structured and full of regulations that there hadn't been room for love. Grace Phillips had clearly done her best to give her children as much of their dreams as she could afford, but the main thing had been that those gifts, however much she'd spent, had been chosen with love.

'What about Christmas with you? Do you have traditions?' Tia asked.

'You've seen the tree in the foyer. That's one of our traditions,' he said. 'Each of the decorations is a special one designed for us by Buschetta—that's a family of jewellers in Casavalle, a bit like Fabergé. The tradition has been going on for more than a century, and there's a secret compartment in each one. Every year, there's a special ceremony to unveil that year's ornament.'

It was about as close as he could get to the special decorations chosen by Tia and her brother each year. Just on a different scale.

'We have Mass in the palace cathedral, and the day after Christmas we open the palace to all the citizens. There's a buffet, with mulled wine and hot chocolate; the palace kitchens bake for days beforehand. Then Luca and I stand at the palace doors with our parents and greet everyone.' Except this year would be different. The first one without his father. The first year with the new King—or Queen. He pushed the thoughts aside. 'There are ice sculptures in the fountain area, and the hedge maze is all lit up for the children to explore. We make sure we give our people a magnificent, beautiful Christmas.'

'I get that you need to do something for your people—like the Queen of England at Sandringham, going to church with her family on Christmas morning and greeting everyone who's queued up outside to see them,' she said. 'But I didn't mean the public stuff. I meant your *private* family Christmas. What about traditions for you? Did you have stockings or anything like that?'

No, they hadn't. Not in the way she meant. 'As royal children,' he said, 'Luca and I had masses of gifts from other royal families and from around the world. To the point where we needed people to help us open them and we didn't always know what people had bought us.'

She frowned. 'You didn't have special things just for you, Luca, your mum and your dad? Not a special story they always read to you, or a film you always watched together?'

'No.'

'That,' she said softly, 'is a shame. Because Christmas isn't about the gifts. It's about love. It's about spending time with your family. Playing games—we'd play everything from snap to charades to snakes and ladders, and I think the best year ever was the year Nathan bought me this game with kazoos where we had to play whatever song was on the card we picked up. We were all terrible at it, Mum and Dad and Nathan and me, and we laughed so much our sides hurt.'

That was something he'd definitely never

done with his family. It was more like the sort of thing he'd done with his army friends. 'That sounds like fun,' he said carefully.

'It was. And I'm sorry you didn't get to share something like that with your family.'

'We had our duties to perform,' he said. Though, now she'd said it, he was sorry, too. He wished he'd been able to share that sort of fun with his parents and his brother.

Would it be different for his baby? If he could persuade Tia to marry him, would she change things at the palace? Would she institute new, more personal, traditions? Would *he* change, too?

The ground felt as if it was shifting under him.

'So did you always want to be in the army?' she asked.

'I'm the younger son, so there weren't quite the same expectations for me as there were for Luca. I had a lot more freedom. And I liked the idea of travelling the world, of being able to make a positive difference for people.'

'Like Nathan,' she said. 'Like our dad.'

'What about you?' he asked.

'I'm fine as I am.'

'No, I mean, what were your dreams when you were young?' He already knew the answer, but he wanted to hear it from her.

'I didn't want to join the army, but I did want to travel,' she said. 'I would've liked to be a primary school teacher, but my grades at school weren't good enough.'

Nathan had always talked about his sister being bright, and Antonio had seen that for himself when he talked to her. He guessed that, as her mother's carer, she'd been too busy to concentrate on her studies at school. 'You could,' he said carefully, 'train as a teacher now. Be a mature student.'

She shook her head. 'Mum suggested that, but I don't want to leave her. And I'm happy as I am. I like my job. My bosses are lovely, and we have regular customers who tell us all kinds of stories of London in the past.'

He had the strongest feeling that Tia was the sort who'd manage to find happiness in any situation: she was one of those incredibly positive people. And she was also incredibly proud and independent. He needed to back off before he upset her. 'OK.'

Once they'd finished dinner, Tia insisted on

helping him to wash up, and then they headed back to the conservatory to watch the stars. Rather than switching on the overhead light, guessing that she'd prefer something softer, Antonio lit the scented pillar candles in their wrought iron and glass lanterns.

'This smells like Christmas,' she said. 'Cinnamon and cloves and orange.'

'I'm glad you like it,' he said. 'Would you like some music?'

'That'd be nice.'

'What do you like?' He knew so little about her.

'Anything.'

'You don't have to be polite,' he said. 'What do you really like listening to? Pop? Classical?'

'This time of year,' she said, 'I really like Christmas music—carols as well as all the old pop songs.'

It didn't take him long to find a medley of Christmas music on a streaming service.

'This is lovely,' she said with a smile. 'All that's missing is the Christmas tree.'

He remembered how her face had lit up when she'd talked to him about the Christmases of her childhood, with her family. Maybe this was a way of getting closer to her. Although he could simply buy everything and have it all shipped in while he took her out for the day tomorrow, he had a feeling that she'd find that much too impersonal—hadn't she said that Christmas for her was all about love and spending time with your family? She'd talked about decorating the tree *together*. So maybe that was what they should do.

'We could have a tree, if you'd like one,' he said. 'Perhaps we can choose one together tomorrow.' He looked at her. 'And maybe we can choose a special decoration for our baby. Together.'

'We're not going to be together, though,' she said softly. 'We come from different worlds.'

'But the baby's part of both of us,' he pointed out. 'The baby's where our worlds combine.'

'I guess,' she said, and there was a hint of sadness in her face.

He wanted to make her feel better. And the only way he could think of was to go and sit beside her on the sofa, and hold both her hands in his. 'It's all going to be OK,' he said.

'I know. I just wish…' She blew out a breath.

'Nathan would've made such a good uncle. Such a good dad. I wish he'd had the chance. But he never talked about anyone special. I'm guessing it was because he felt responsible for Mum and me so he didn't let himself get close to anyone.'

Antonio thought that was a shrewd assessment. But it was only part of the truth. 'He loved you both,' Antonio told her. 'He didn't see either of you as a burden. He was so proud of you.'

'I was proud of him. So was Mum. And I wish Dad could've seen him grow up past the age of thirteen—and me past the age of ten.' She looked at him. 'I'm sorry. This must be hard for you, too, right now. Your first Christmas without your father.'

He nodded. 'It's…a little strange.'

Her fingers tightened around his, giving him comfort. 'The firsts are hard. Your first birthday without him, his birthday, Christmas, the first anniversary of his death. But he's still in your heart. Always. That never changes.'

But Antonio's relationship with his family was very different from hers. Duty came before everything else. And, like the rest of his family, he didn't allow himself to think about feelings.

Right now, here in the cosy warmth of the room, with Christmas music playing in the background, the view of the mountains lit by moonlight, and the soft glow of the candles illuminating her face, he felt different. As if something was unfurling inside him and spreading through him, something that made him feel warm and mushy and very mixed-up, all at the same time. And he didn't know how to tell her how he felt, just in case he was making a fool of himself and she didn't feel the same. After all, this was the woman who'd refused to marry him—even though she was pregnant with his child. Instead, he said, 'Will you dance with me?'

She blinked. 'Dance with you? I...'

Of course she didn't want that. He was expecting way too much from her. 'Sorry. I shouldn't have asked.' He let her hands go.

'It's not that. Just...' She looked wistful. 'Dancing isn't really something I've done very much.'

No, because when she wasn't working she was looking after her mum. She probably wouldn't have gone out to discos at school, or nightclubs, or the kind of glitzy social events he went to. But if her not knowing how to dance was the only barrier between them, he could fix that. Right here, right now. The words spilled out before he could stop them. 'I can teach you.'

'Teach me?'

And suddenly it was as if there was a kind of electricity in the air. Something that made it hard to breathe.

Would she let him closer? Or would she make an excuse and back away?

Waiting for her answer made time seem to slow down; every second felt ten times as long as usual, as if he was watching a film in slow motion.

But then she nodded. 'OK.'

He drew her to her feet. In bare feet, she was more than six inches shorter than he was, and it made him feel even more protective of her.

'OK. Follow my lead.'

Michael Bublé crooned 'Have Yourself a Merry Little Christmas' as Antonio swayed with Tia in the candlelight. And he rested his cheek against her hair, feeling the softness against his skin and breathing in her light floral scent.

With Antonio's arms wrapped protectively round her, Tia felt safer than she'd felt for a long, long time. It was amazing to be dancing in his arms by candlelight, to the kind of Christmas music she loved most. It felt as if the room was lit by a thousand stars, and she'd always thought herself a bit clumsy, but right now she was dancing effortlessly in his arms, not putting a foot wrong because he was guiding her.

Just for a moment, she could let herself believe this was real. That he was holding her, not because he was being polite and doing his duty but because he really wanted her—her and their baby. That he *cared*.

But then the music changed and a choir began to sing 'Silent Night'.

Her mother's favourite.

Homesickness washed over her. She missed her mum; she worried about Grace constantly. And Antonio had hit the nail very firmly on the head earlier. Just how was she going to cope with working part time, looking after their baby and looking after her mum? Right at that moment the future felt filled with anxiety.

As if Antonio sensed her tension, he pulled back. 'Everything's going to be OK, Tia,' he said softly.

It was, oh, so easy to say; and much less easy to be sure that it was true. 'Uh-huh,' she said, not wanting him to think she was feeble and weak, or that she wanted to give up and let him sort everything out for her. Because that wasn't who she was. She managed. She always had.

'You've had a very long day and you've done a lot of travelling,' he said. 'Let me run you a bath and make you some hot chocolate.'

Tia was perfectly capable of running her own bath.

But, at the same time, she was bone-deep tired. And he was right: she'd had a long day and a lot of travelling. She'd been on three planes, two cars and a train. And she was six months pregnant. She had more than herself to think about: there was the baby, too. Just this once, maybe it wouldn't hurt to let him look after her. Right now she was his guest, and you looked after your guests, didn't you? 'Thank you. That'd be really kind.' She gave him a grateful smile.

Antonio was almost surprised that she'd given in so easily. Then again, she was six months pregnant and it had been a long day. He wasn't going to make a big deal about this, and then hopefully it would soften her stance and she would let him do more to help.

Though he had no idea what kind of form that help could take. Tia Phillips was independent to a fault.

Again and again, the only thing he could come back to was that they should get married. She was expecting his baby. A baby who was fourth in line to the throne of Casavalle. It was the honourable thing to do. The right solution. He could look after her, look after the baby, and look after her mother.

Though she'd made it clear that she'd only get married for love.

Did he love her?

They hardly knew each other. He wasn't even sure that he believed in love, let alone love at first sight; how did you even know how love felt? How did you know someone was 'the one'? How did you know it would last?

As a prince, he couldn't afford to risk a relationship that might go wrong and make things awkward for his family. Duty always came first.

And yet... There was something about Tia that drew him. He liked her. He enjoyed her company. He was definitely attracted to her. So that was a start. Somehow, over the next three days, he needed to make her happy and show her that this could work out. That they could have a proper partnership. Work as a team. Learn to love each other, if that was what she wanted.

Once she was back downstairs, clad in pyjamas and with her hair wrapped in a towel, he settled her on the sofa in the living room with a mug of hot milk and a fleecy blanket. 'It must've been hard for you growing up, losing your dad and with your mum ill.'

'We managed,' Tia said. 'Mum took in sewing and mending and she worked from home, so she could rest when she needed to.'

And he'd just bet that Tia had picked up the slack. Now he thought about it, Nathan had been good with a needle, too. No doubt he'd also helped with their mother's work.

'Nathan got a job at the corner shop working weekends, and I had a paper round,' Tia explained. 'I took over at the shop when he joined the army. The manager was brilliant—she knew the situation with Mum, so she'd let me nip home to check on Mum if she was having a bad day. Between us, Nathan and I sorted the housework when Mum couldn't do it.'

Meaning that Tia had had to do it all on her own after her brother joined the army. It was so far away from Antonio's own life of privilege, and he really admired Tia's strength. And Nathan's, too; although his friend had never confided much about his past, he'd had amazing strength of character.

'It must've been tough, though. What about school?'

She shrugged. 'I got by.'

But not, he thought, with the kind of grades her brother thought she was capable of. Even if you were bright, if you were caring for someone else you simply wouldn't have time to keep up with your schoolwork and your grades would suffer. He could see how Tia's dreams of travelling and becoming a primary school teacher just hadn't been possible.

'Don't judge my mum,' she said softly. 'If the authorities had known how ill Mum was and how much help we needed to give her, they might've taken us away from her and put us in care—and they probably would have made Nathan and me live with different families. That happened to someone in my class and I was terrified that it would happen to me. I didn't want to be taken away from Mum and Nathan, and he didn't want to leave Mum and me, either. So we just got on with things and made sure the teachers and everyone didn't really know how ill Mum was. It was fine, because we had each other and we were together.'

This was so much worse than Antonio had realised, and his heart ached for Nathan and his equally brave little sister. 'You didn't have any family who could help? Any grandparents?'

'Mum was an only child, and her parents died before I was born,' Tia said. 'And Dad's family didn't like my mum. There was a big row when they first got together, and they never made it up. Nathan wrote to them after Dad died, but they never replied. But it's OK.' She spread her hands and smiled. 'You don't miss what you've never had. And my mum's brilliant. Even when she's having a really bad day, she never complains. She's the kindest, most loving mum anyone could ask for and I'm really grateful I have her.'

Guilt flooded through him. 'I'm sorry I haven't been there to support you both since Nathan died.'

'*Support* us? Mum and I don't need your money, Your Royal Highness,' she said crisply. 'We're not a charity case.'

He looked at her, horrified to realise she thought that he'd meant money. 'Of course you're not, and I wouldn't insult you by treating you that way.' He knew she was proud. Offering her money would be the quickest way to put a barrier up between them.

'I'm sorry,' she said, and bit her lip. 'I shouldn't have snapped at you. Just… I guess I've learned that rich people tend to think about everything in terms of money.'

'And, as a prince, I'm from a very wealthy background, so it figures you'd think I'd be even more that way,' he said grimly. 'Though I didn't mean money. I meant I should've come back and given you some emotional support—you *and* your mother. And instead I disappeared and just left you to it.'

'You told me you weren't at Nathan's funeral because you had to go on another mission, and then your dad died so you had responsibilities in your own family. Of course you didn't have time to come and support us. And I apologise. I didn't mean to insult you just now by implying…' She grimaced. 'I suppose it sounded as if I thought that you were trying to buy my silence.'

'But you must've felt that I'd abandoned you when I didn't come back and see you.'

'Not so much me—I was angry with you for my mum's sake,' Tia admitted. 'I thought it wouldn't have been that much of a sacrifice for you just to spend a few minutes with her, sharing your memories of my brother. Or send her a photograph or a personal note or something. Just so she knew he mattered.'

'He did matter. He mattered a lot.' Antonio raked a hand through his hair. 'And you're right, I should have made the time to do that. I handled it badly when I came to see you. I'm sorry I got it so wrong.'

'And I'm sorry for going off at the deep end,' she said, and the sweetness in her smile ripped his heart in two.

'I think,' he said, 'we could both do with an early night. In separate rooms,' he added hastily. 'There are no strings to you staying here.'

'I'm a bit tired,' she admitted.

'We'll talk again in the morning,' he said. And, just so she'd know he didn't make promises lightly, he added, 'And then we can go and get that tree.'

'OK,' she said.

He took her empty mug from her and washed up before heading to bed, but he lay awake for a long time before he finally fell asleep.

Would Tia trust him enough to let her support him?

And, if not, how could he teach her to trust him?

He really needed to think things through properly before tomorrow. He couldn't afford to get this wrong.

CHAPTER FOUR

THE NEXT MORNING, when Tia woke, she felt slightly disoriented. It was strange not to hear the low hum of traffic that she was used to, and even stranger to be lying in a wide bed instead of her narrow single bed. She glanced at her watch, and realised it was a quarter past seven; normally she'd have been up for nearly an hour, getting ready to help her mum and then go to work.

Then again, London was an hour behind Casavalle, so this was pretty much the normal time for her to wake and she wasn't late. Though maybe, given the time zone difference, it was a little too early to ring her mother in London and see how she was.

Tia climbed out of bed and looked out of the window. The sky was streaked with pink and gold. As she watched, the snow on the mountains gradually turned pink. So pretty, and such a lovely way to start the day.

But this wasn't how her life was going to be, so she wasn't going to let herself get used to it.

She showered swiftly and dressed in one of the silky long-sleeved tops and the maternity trousers Antonio's housekeeper had bought for her. The fabric was so soft against her skin and felt so nice.

Tears pricked at her eyelids, and she grew cross with herself. It was utterly ridiculous, starting to cry over a complete stranger being so kind to her.

'Get a grip,' she told herself. 'You're here for three days and you need to sort out a compromise with the Prince.'

There was no sound in the house, so she crept quietly down the stairs and into the kitchen to make herself a mug of tea. She thought about making a mug of tea for Antonio, but that would mean taking the mug into his room and she felt too shy to do that. How ridiculous that was, given that she was carrying his baby; but he was almost a complete stranger. They were worlds apart. She was a waitress, living in a tiny flat in a very ordinary part of London, and he was a prince who lived in an enormous fairy-tale palace in the middle of the Mediterranean. He wouldn't fit into her life and she wouldn't fit into his.

The problem was she'd felt so close to him last night, when she'd told him about Christmases in the past with her family. It was her favourite time of year—not because of the gifts but because it was a chance to spend time with those you loved, enjoying their company and having fun together.

It sounded as if fun hadn't been part of Antonio's Christmases, growing up. Everything had been so formal and stuffy. All the priceless and historic ornaments on the tree that couldn't be played with in case they were accidentally broken: things that had to be admired from afar. Receiving gifts from people he might never even have met, and gifts he probably didn't get a chance to play with. Standing to greet the citizens and doing his royal duties instead of playing games with his family.

His family.

How could they ever accept someone like her? Someone who didn't have blue blood; someone who didn't have the first clue about protocol and royal etiquette.

So she needed to keep a lid on the attraction

she felt towards Antonio Valenti. She needed to ignore the impulse to wrap her arms round him and hold him close when she thought about how lonely his childhood must have been, because this really wasn't her place.

She'd promised him a couple of days to talk things over. She'd keep her promise. And then she'd depart quietly for London and leave all this behind her.

With her hands wrapped round the mug of tea, she walked into the conservatory and curled up in one of the big armchairs, enjoying the beautiful view. At least this was a memory she could share with her baby in years to come.

If only she could share it with Antonio, too.

But he didn't love her, and she wasn't prepared to commit to a life with him without love—for her or for her baby.

She'd promised him three days. Antonio really hoped that would be enough to talk her round to his point of view.

He decided to start by bringing Tia a cup of tea in bed, and then possibly bring her a breakfast tray. Then they'd go into the village and find a Christmas tree together, and choose some ornaments. They'd spend the afternoon decorating the tree. And he could drop hints that this was something they could do with their baby. They could follow her family traditions and there would be a new one from a shop every year, and a home-made one.

It was almost the total opposite of the Buschetta ornament tradition that he was used to. But if Tia wanted things handmade and personal, that was exactly what he'd give her. And, even though he couldn't ever remember sitting down with glitter and glue, he was quite prepared to do that. He'd do whatever it took to make her happy and believe in him. Because maybe, just maybe, Tia and the baby were going to change his life. Fill in the gaps. Just as he could fill in the gaps of her life. He'd thought that these three days were to persuade her, but his feelings towards her had already started to change. She wasn't just the unexpected mother of his baby, the woman he had a duty towards; he was starting to really enjoy the time he spent with her.

He showered and changed into a pair of black jeans and a cashmere sweater, then headed down to the kitchen.

Except, when he went to fill the kettle, he realised that it was still hot.

So did that mean Tia was already up and about? She'd liked the view from the conservatory yesterday, he remembered, so he went in search of her. And there she was, curled up in a chair, sipping tea and looking out at the mountains.

'Good morning,' he said.

And how weird it was that his pulse had leaped at the sight of her. She looked so cute sitting there in a half-dream, with her dark curls caught back at the nape of her neck. She didn't need make-up to emphasise those beautiful brown eyes, either.

This was more than attraction. Antonio kept circling round to the L-word in his head, but love wasn't something that he believed in or could even define. In royal circles, you didn't marry for love; you married for duty and for dynastic reasons. His father had made that mistake in his first marriage, falling in love with someone who couldn't cope with the Royal life that came with him.

Being with Tia, marrying her, was really going to put the cat among the pigeons, politically.

Or maybe this would take his life in a new direction. A better direction. Because being with her made him feel that there could be something more than duty and work in his life. Something he hadn't expected or looked for, but now he'd had a glimpse of it he wanted more. And he definitely wanted that for their baby.

'Good morning,' she said, smiling back at him. 'I hope it was OK for me to make myself some tea.'

'Of course. Please treat the house as your home,' he said.

'I was going to make you a mug, too, but I wasn't sure if you'd be awake yet.'

There was a shyness in her smile that really drew him.

And then he noticed the bump moving; he could see her silky top shimmering in the light. 'Is that…?' he asked.

'The baby kicking? Yes.' She looked at him, then held her hand out. 'Here. Feel it for your-self.'

He let her take his hand and rest it on the bump.

This felt oddly intimate. Strange. He could hardly breathe.

'Say hello to the baby,' she said.

'Hello, baby,' he whispered.

Immediately, there was a strong kick against his hand, as if the baby was saying hello back, and it blew him away. He really hadn't expected to feel that sudden rush of wonder.

'Our baby just kicked me!' He dragged in a breath. Now it felt real.

Of course it was real.

For pity's sake, anyone who looked at Tia could see that she was six months pregnant.

But for the first time Antonio felt as if he'd actually connected with the baby. A baby he hadn't expected, hadn't ever dreamed about— and now he discovered that he really, really wanted this baby. It was a sudden, unexpected, visceral longing, stronger than anything he'd known before.

And it made him look at Tia differently, too. She was the mother of his child. And although he'd been telling himself that they barely knew each other so they couldn't possibly feel any-thing for each other, now he realised that he'd been totally in denial. Because he did feel things for her. More than just physical attraction. This went deeper. He didn't have the words for it and it scared the hell out of him because he'd never felt anything like this before. All he knew was that he wanted her. Her and the baby.

That kick just now made him even more determined that this would work out.

'Can the baby hear me talking?' he asked.

She nodded. 'He likes being talked to. He really likes it when Mum sings to him.'

Singing to an unborn baby. He'd never thought of doing something like that. 'What, like a lullaby or something?'

She smiled. 'Pop songs. The Beatles, Take That, the Beach Boys. And we watched *Love Actually* again last weekend—Mum and I watch it every Christmas. He kicked like mad to "Catch a Falling Star" and "All I Want for Christmas is You".' She grinned. 'Probably because Mum and I were singing along, too.'

Singing to a baby.

He had so much to learn.

Would she have the patience to teach him?

'Does he—she—our baby,' he amended, 'kick at certain times?'

'He's usually quite lively first thing in the morning,' she said. 'And he's taken to doing somersaults at two in the morning. Mum says that's probably when he's going to wake up, wanting milk.'

'Our baby,' Antonio whispered.

Antonio's face was full of wonder. And was that a catch in his voice, a shimmer of tears in his eyes as he connected with their child?

For a moment, Tia was filled with hope.

Maybe he'd been right to bring her here. Maybe spending time together would help make the future clearer. Talking about their dreams, their hopes, what they wanted for the baby. Getting to know each other properly— their real selves—would help them find a way forward. Not in the daily grind of London, not in the unreal glamour of the palace, but here in the mountains—the place he'd loved since he was a child and came back to when he needed a breathing space. Here, where Antonio could be himself instead of being what he thought the world expected a prince to be.

'I never expected...' For a moment, his hand curved protectively over the bump. And then he grimaced and pulled his hand away. 'I apologise. That was intrusive of me.'

He was worried about touching her? Considering that they'd made a baby together… On the other hand, he'd been brought up with the strictest of protocols, and his job meant following rules and regulations, too. 'Most people like feeling a baby kick,' she said. 'Perfect strangers come up to me sometimes and ask if they can feel the baby kick.'

He looked surprised, as if it was something that had never occurred to him before.

'And this is your baby,' she added softly. 'It's absolutely fine for you to put your hand on my bump and feel him kick whenever you want to.'

He still didn't look comfortable with the idea. What would it take to make him unbend completely? she wondered.

'Can I get you some breakfast?' he asked.

'Toast would be lovely. Or fruit and yogurt. Whatever you have.'

'I'll call you when breakfast is ready,' he promised.

The toast was perfect, and there was a choice of local honey and jam.

'Would you like to go and choose a tree this morning?' he asked.

She wrinkled her nose at him. 'It seems a

little bit extravagant, buying a tree for just a couple of days.'

'I'd like to give you a sort of Christmas in Casavalle,' he said.

Start some memories that they could share with the baby one day? Tia didn't say it out loud, in case she was wrong. But that moment when Antonio had first felt their baby kick, when his eyes had been full of joy and wonder, gave her hope that maybe he could break through the constriction of his upbringing. And if he could unbend, if he really was the man she was beginning to get to know, then maybe they really did have a future together. Maybe they really could be a team and have the kind of relationship her parents had had: the one thing she'd longed for so much but had thought would never happen. And the hope burned, so clear and so bright, in her heart.

'All right,' she said. 'Let's buy a tree. As long as it's a small one.'

Decorating the streets for Christmas seemed to be in full swing when they walked into the village together. There were nativity scenes in every shop window, each slightly different;

there was a Christmas tree made out of wine bottles in the wine shop, a nativity scene with a backdrop of beautiful silk scarves in a boutique, another made from spun sugar in a confectionery store, and another made entirely from teddy bears in the toy shop.

'This is all amazing,' she said. 'So creative.'

'The shop windows are incredible,' he agreed. 'Displaying the nativity scene in shop windows has been a tradition here for many years, like it is in mainland Italy.'

Once they'd finished enjoying the displays, he said, 'Let's go and choose our tree. What would you like?'

Thinking of the scarily large tree at the palace, she said, 'Nothing taller than you.'

He grinned and pointed out the massive tree that had just been put up in the central square. 'Not like that, then? Because that might just fit.'

For a moment, remembering the double-height hallway in his house, she wondered if he was serious; then the glint in his eyes made her realise that he was teasing her. Something she hadn't expected, and which reinforced her hope for the future.

Not to mention how cute he was. That little

quirk at the corner of his mouth. It made her
want to stand on tiptoe, wrap her arms round
his neck and steal a kiss.

What would he do if she did that?

Would it be too much, too soon? Would he
push her away? Or would he wrap his arms
tightly round her and kiss her all the way back?

She didn't dare take the risk. Not until she
had a better idea of what he was thinking.

Instead, she kept the conversation light. Decorating was a safe subject. And she wasn't
going to mention mistletoe.

'I'd prefer a little tree,' she said with a smile.
'Do you normally decorate the house here?'

'No,' he admitted. 'We're expected to be
at the palace from the middle of November.
It seems a bit pointless to decorate the house
without anyone being here to enjoy it.'

'So do you actually have any decorations for
the tree?'

'No. I thought maybe we could choose them
together.'

Start a new tradition together, perhaps? But
she suppressed the hope before it could take
hold.

They headed for the pop-up Christmas stalls

in the market place, and finally found the tree with the perfect shape and the perfect height. Antonio paid for it and arranged to have it delivered to the house later that morning.

The baby seemed to be kicking more at the sound of Antonio's voice. Recognising his father, perhaps?

At another of the stalls, Tia was really taken with a fir wreath that had seed pods of honesty sprayed with copper paint threaded through it. 'That's so pretty,' she said. 'I must remember to suggest that to Mum. She always makes the wreath for our front door. Maybe I can ask if they'd mind me taking a photograph.'

'I have a better solution. Would you like this one for the house?' he asked.

'I...' She looked at him. 'Would that be all right?'

'If it makes you happy, it makes me happy,' he said softly. 'And by buying here in the Christmas market I'm supporting the local economy, which is a good thing.'

So everybody won. 'Thank you. That would be really lovely,' she said.

Once they'd finished strolling around the stalls, Antonio steered her into a café. 'Until you've tried the hot chocolate here,' he said, 'you haven't tasted perfection.'

The hot chocolate was thick and rich, yet less sweet than the sort she'd drink back in England, and it was teamed perfectly with a slice of white chocolate and lemon *panettone*.

'Sorry, I'm afraid I need the ladies',' she said when she'd finished her hot chocolate.

'I've been reading up,' Antonio said. 'I gather it's a pregnant woman thing, especially in the third trimester.'

She nodded ruefully. 'I'm afraid so.'

On her way to the toilets, she saw a notice about the village children's Christmas party in the town hall. She didn't think anything of it until she was washing her hands and two women came in, both looking anxious and speaking in rapid Italian.

'I can't believe Mario went skiing yesterday and managed to break his leg. Whatever was my brother thinking? He was supposed to dress up as Father Christmas tomorrow afternoon for the children's party. He can't possibly do it now, not with his leg in plaster,' one of them said.

'Of course not. Poor man.'

'Oh, I don't pity him too much. He knew we

were relying on him, but he had to go and show off on the slopes.' The first woman rolled her eyes. 'But now we have to find another Father Christmas, and everyone I've asked has a prior commitment they can't break.'

'We can't let the children down,' the second woman said.

'I'll keep going through my phone book, but I'm beginning to think we need some kind of Christmas miracle to find a new *Babbo Natale*,' the first woman said.

Or maybe they just needed an incognito prince, Tia thought. Antonio didn't have any prior commitments tomorrow at the palace; he'd arranged to spend a couple of days here with her, and she was perfectly happy for him to spend some of that time playing Father Christmas for the children. She almost opened her mouth and suggested it, but a kick from the baby stayed her.

Perhaps she really ought to check with Antonio first before she offered his services as *Babbo Natale*. Would he even be allowed to do something like that? And, if he was allowed to, would he want to, or was she expecting too much of him?

She looked at the poster again on her way back to the table, and took a photograph of it on her phone. If she could persuade Antonio into the Christmas spirit this afternoon, when they decorated his Christmas tree, then maybe he would agree to help save the children's Christmas party and arrange it with his security team.

Antonio had just had the perfect idea for the next stage of persuading Tia to give them a chance. What went with a Christmas tree better than a Christmas dinner?

A full-blown traditional Italian Christmas Eve dinner might be a little rich for a pregnant woman, he thought. But maybe he could cook her a traditional English dinner, the sort she'd shared with her family when she was young. The sort Nathan had told him about, with crispy roast potatoes, Brussels sprouts, sausages wrapped in bacon and, most of all, a huge roasted turkey.

And, with a little help, he could make this a nice surprise for her. He knew he could look up what he needed to know, but there was a quicker way to deal with this—and he needed to get this organised right now, before Tia came back to their table.

He grabbed his phone from his pocket and called Gina, the housekeeper who looked after the place when they weren't there.

'Good morning, Prince Antonio,' she answered. 'How are you?'

'I'm fine, thank you, Gina. And how are you?' he said politely.

'*Bene, grazie*,' she said, and he could hear the smile in her voice. 'Is there something you need me to do for you?'

'I was wondering… How long does it take to cook a traditional English roast turkey?'

'A turkey? It depends on the size.'

'For Christmas dinner, I was thinking a big one.'

'A six-kilogram turkey would take just under four hours to cook, plus half an hour to rest,' Gina mused.

He glanced at his watch. 'That would be perfect. Would you be able to source one for me and get it delivered to the house, please?'

'Of course, Prince Antonio.'

'And I need a few other things, too, please.' He rattled off the things he remembered Nathan talking about. 'And finally a Christmas pudding.'

'An English one?'

'An English one,' he confirmed.

'Now, that,' Gina said, 'will be a problem. A home-made one has to be made at least a month in advance so it can mature. And none of the shops in Picco Innevato is likely to stock an English Christmas pudding. Your best option for that, perhaps, is to have one flown in—either from Rome or from London.'

Which would be expensive. Money wasn't a problem for him but he knew it was a problem for Tia. Antonio was pretty sure she would react badly if he spent so much money on something as frivolous and extravagant as having a Christmas pudding flown in from London. And what if she didn't actually like Christmas pudding? 'What could I make as an alternative?'

'Perhaps a jelly, something that you can serve with fresh fruit and biscuits,' Gina said. 'Or perhaps some traditional Italian Christmas doughnuts.' She paused. 'Prince Antonio, I know I'm stepping outside the boundaries, but may I ask *why* you want to cook an English Christmas dinner?'

'I want to do something nice for my best friend's sister,' Antonio said. 'And I'd like to surprise her with it this evening.'

'Then why not make the meal a mixture of English and Casavallian traditions?' Gina suggested. 'So then you can have ravioli or gnocchi for a starter, the turkey and all the traditional English trimmings for the main, and then an Italian pudding and cheeses to finish?'

'That's a really good idea,' Antonio said. 'Thank you.'

'Your best friend's sister. Hmm. Would this be the same lady I bought the maternity clothes for?' Gina asked.

'Yes, and she loved them. Thank you again for your help,' Antonio said.

'It was my pleasure. And I will organise your turkey,' Gina said. 'Since you want to surprise her, you need to keep away from the house for long enough for me to get everything bought and delivered. Give me, say, two hours. Shall I prepare and cook everything for you?'

That would be the easy way out. He rather thought he needed to make the effort himself, if he was to impress Tia. 'Thank you, but I want to cook it myself. I'd appreciate a note about the

turkey, though. I can handle everything else.'
Or he could look it up online.

'*Bene.* I will arrange everything, and I will text you when I'm done,' Gina said.

'Thank you, Gina. I really appreciate your help,' he said.

He could see Tia walking back to their table, so he ended the call swiftly and pretended he'd simply been looking at something on his phone.

'Is everything all right?' he asked.

'Yes, thank you.'

Now all he had to do was to keep her away from the house for a couple of hours.

'Shall we go and look for decorations?' he asked.

'Of course. Do you want a particular colour scheme?'

Like the ones in the palace? He had a feeling that she'd like something a lot more informal. 'This will be my first Christmas tree all of my own,' he said. 'So I'm happy to hear your suggestions.'

'Let's see what they have in the shops and what you like,' she suggested.

'What do you need for a tree?' he asked.

'Lights, maybe tinsel, something for the

top of the tree and some ornaments,' she said promptly.

Lights turned out to be incredibly complicated.

'First of all, do you want white lights or coloured ones?' she asked when they were in the middle of one of the shops.

'Do you have a preference?' he asked.

'I like white ones,' she admitted. 'So they look like the stars.'

'Then we'll have white ones.'

But then it was about choosing string lights or LED lights; warm white or ice white; and did they want lights that twinkled, or glowed, or flashed, or moved in a pattern, or came with sound effects?

He didn't actually care, but he did need Tia out of the house so Gina could organise the ingredients for his surprise Christmas dinner, so he pretended to be much more interested in all the different functions than he really was. Ordering Tia about simply wouldn't work. He knew from his army days that if your team felt they had a stake in things and you were listening to them, they'd go above and beyond the call of duty for you.

They'd do this together. The personal way. So Tia would be sure he'd listened to her and wanted to work with her instead of imposing his Royal will. He'd prove to her that they were a good team. And then perhaps she would agree to marry him and the baby would have his protection.

Once they'd chosen the lights, they wandered into the decorations department. Antonio paid close attention to the things she passed over and the things she seemed to like. In the end she chose silver and blue baubles, filigree silver stars, blue tinsel and a large silver star for the top of the tree.

She paused by the stand of glass baubles; there was a special one etched with a picture of the mountain and the words '*Picco Innevato 2019*'.

Hadn't she said that she, her parents and Nathan had chosen a new, special decoration together each year?

He was fairly sure from her expression that she really liked the glass bauble. He was also fairly sure that she thought it was way too much money for one little decoration.

'May I buy this for...?' He paused, getting the

strongest feeling that she'd say no if he asked to buy it for her. But for the baby, perhaps...

'For our baby?' he said.

She nodded, and he thought he could see the sudden sparkle of tears in her eyes. Oh, no. He hadn't meant to upset her. 'Are you all right?' he asked.

'Yes. It's just...'

Part of her family tradition that would never be the same again, because her brother was no longer with them. He knew how that felt.

'It's a new beginning,' he said softly. 'We can't share this Christmas with Nathan or my father. But we can still share it with others. My new sister. Our baby.'

'Yes,' she said, and this time a single tear really did slide down her cheek.

He brushed it away with the pad of his thumb. Funny how such a light contact sent a shard of desire through him.

He needed to be more careful. This wasn't about his feelings. It was about doing the right thing. The honourable thing. His duty. He was beginning to think that they might just be in the same direction. Tia Phillips made him feel all kinds of things he'd never felt before. It was unsettling, yet at the same time it made him want to explore further, discover what it was about her that roused all his instincts: protectiveness, desire and…

He didn't quite have a name for the emotion, or at least he wasn't ready to admit it, even to himself. But he did know he wanted Tia around. And this wasn't like his past relationships, strictly for fun and only for now. He wanted more. He wanted all the warmth and the sweetness she could bring to his life.

When they'd finished in the decoration shop, he managed to stall her by insisting on having lunch out at one of the cafés in the village. Even though he'd made it very clear that this was his treat, he noticed that she picked the cheapest thing on the menu, and his heart bled for her.

If only she'd let him cherish her, the way she deserved.

But he was pretty sure she'd see it as an attack on her independence.

Finally, his phone buzzed to signal a message; he glanced at it surreptitiously, relieved to see that it was from Gina.

All done. Turkey in fridge, in roasting tin and foil, ready to go in oven.

She'd added cooking times and temperatures, too.

So Operation Persuade Tia could go full steam ahead.

As soon as Tia headed for the toilets, he texted Gina back.

Thank you.

He'd make very sure to arrange for a delivery of flowers this afternoon to show his gratitude properly. Even though it was Gina's job to look after the house and the family's needs when they were in residence, she was going the extra mile because he'd asked her to, and he wanted her to know he appreciated it.

Back at his house, he asked Tia, 'Where do you want to put the tree?'

'It's your family house, so it's your decision,' she reminded him.

'It's our Christmas,' he countered. 'So tell me what you want.'

'Could we put it in the conservatory?' she asked.

He'd half expected her to say that. He knew how much she loved the view from there. 'Of course,' he said.

While she set out the decorations, he put the Christmas tree up in the conservatory.

And maybe letting her be in charge of the decorating was the way forward, he thought. It would show her that he wouldn't insist on everything being done *his* way.

'So how do you want to do this?' he asked when she came to stand beside him.

'Start with the lights. Check they work, first.'

That was blatantly obvious—before you drove a car or flew a plane, you checked the lights worked—but he wasn't going to snap at her. She seemed to be enjoying the fact that he was deferring to her experience in Christmas-tree decorating. And he rather liked this confident side of her, so he just smiled and plugged them in. 'All present and correct.'

'So then we start at the top, weaving them in and out of the branches as we work our way down. It's probably easiest if we stand either side of the tree and feed the lights round to each other,' she said.

Antonio enjoyed that. Particularly when his fingers brushed against hers when they transferred the lights to each other, and she blushed.

So she wasn't that indifferent to him, then…

Maybe, like him, she wasn't quite ready to put a name to what she was feeling. And maybe they'd find the courage to admit it—together.

Deliberately he let his fingers brush against hers again. And he held her gaze when she looked up at him. Her mouth was very slightly parted. Soft. Sweet. Tempting.

He remembered what it felt like to kiss her.

He wanted to kiss her again.

Yet, at the same time, he didn't want to push her too fast. These three days were supposed to be all about getting to know each other, spending time together, and talking. Kissing her meant that they wouldn't be talking. Not talking meant that they wouldn't be able to sort things out. So he resisted the urge. Though he noticed that she was staring at his mouth, too. Was she, too, remembering what it had felt like to kiss? To touch?

He nearly dropped a bauble at the thought, but he kept himself under control, the way he always did—both as a prince and as a soldier. Because he was going to do this the right way. Slowly. Well, as slowly as you could get in the three days she'd promised him.

When they'd finished, she turned on the lights and walked round the tree. 'That's great. No dark patches or gaps. Now we can put the star on the top.'

'Don't you do that last?' he asked.

She shook her head. 'Mum always said to work top down.' Her smile was wistful. 'Nathan and I used to take turns in putting the star on the top. Dad would lift us up, even when Nathan was twelve and getting really tall. But we were too big for Mum to lift us after Dad died, so then we used to stand on a chair.'

What would she do if he lifted her up? Would she back away? Or would she melt into his arms? Both options made him nervous. And, although he wanted to show her that they had a future, he didn't want her to feel that he was railroading her into things. He wanted her to want this, too.

He looked at her. 'Your choice. Chair or...?'

Was she going to choose him, or would she pick the safe option?

'Chair,' she said.

The safe option, then. He needed to back off. 'Chair,' he repeated, and fetched one. 'Though I'd prefer you to hold my shoulder for balance.'

She smiled, then. 'From the kick I just got, I think someone agrees with you.'

'Good. Our baby's sensible, then,' he said lightly.

Even though he knew she was only holding on to him for balance as she climbed up and he was careful not to breach any boundaries, his skin still tingled through his sweater where her hand rested on his shoulder. What he really wanted to do was to wrap his arms round her, kiss the bump, and then lift her down from the chair so he could kiss her... But still he kept himself in check. Just.

Once she'd climbed down again, he helped her add the tinsel garland, the baubles and the snowflakes, and then finally the special glass bauble for the baby. Again, his hands brushed against hers, and this time when he turned to her he noticed that her lips were slightly parted and her pupils were enormous.

All he had to do was lean forward and brush his mouth against hers.

She held his gaze for a moment, glanced at his mouth and then up again.

His heart skipped a beat as she closed her eyes.

Now...

He'd closed half the gap between them when the alarm on his phone shrilled.

Her eyes opened again and she stared at him in shock.

Talk about *timing*. 'Sorry,' he said. 'That's my schedule.'

'Schedule?'

'Uh-huh. I need to do something in the kitchen.'

So much for thinking that he was going to get away with this, because she followed him into the kitchen. 'You've got an alarm on your phone to tell you to do something in here?'

'Yes.' He sighed. 'Since you're clearly not going to budge until I tell you, I need to put the turkey in the oven.'

'What turkey?'

'The turkey we're eating tonight. I'm cooking you Christmas dinner.'

'You're cooking me Christmas dinner?' she echoed, blinking at him with surprise.

Oh, honestly. Just because he was a prince,

it didn't mean he was incapable of doing anything. He could dress himself, too. The years of royals needing valets and lady's maids had gone long, long ago. And he'd made her dinner last night. 'I *can* cook, you know,' he said, slightly exasperated. 'Putting alarms on my phone means I know when to put things in the oven and when to check them or take them out.'

'You're cooking me Christmas dinner,' she repeated. And this time she smiled. 'I really didn't expect that.'

'It's not a completely traditional English Christmas dinner. It's a fusion,' he said. 'In Casavalle, traditionally we have fish on Christmas Eve. The meal can be eight or nine courses.'

She rubbed her bump. 'I'm not sure I'd be able to manage that much.'

'And some of it's spicy. So that's why I'm cooking a fusion meal,' he said. 'I remember Nathan talking about turkey and the trimmings, so I'm cooking that. I don't have time to soak the salt cod to make *baccalà* for a first course, so I'm doing traditional gnocchi with sage and butter sauce instead—well, I admit it's not home-made and comes from the deli— and an Italian pudding, because the only way

I'd get a traditional English Christmas pudding here is to fly one in.'

She frowned. 'Fly one in? That's crazy—it's a total waste of money. You could use that to do something better.' She spread her hands. 'Say, something nice for the villagers here in Picco Innevato.'

'I thought you might react like that,' he said, 'so I'm not flying a pudding in. I'm making *frittelle*—fried Christmas doughnuts. But you're putting me off my schedule. Can you just—well—not talk for five minutes?' he asked plaintively.

She gave him a speaking look, but nodded.

He took the turkey out of the fridge.

'That's enormous!' Tia protested.

So much for her not speaking for five minutes. 'Isn't that the point of a Christmas turkey, to be enormous?' he asked, putting the bird into the oven.

'We'll never eat all that, even if you can talk Giacomo into eating with us this evening,' she said. 'And how did you get this anyway? It wasn't in the fridge when I got the milk out this morning.'

'I called Gina while we were in the café,' he admitted, 'and she organised this for us.'

'Then perhaps you can invite Gina to share Christmas dinner with us,' Tia suggested. 'Does she have a family?'

'Yes. She lives with her husband. Her children are grown up now, and they live in the capital rather than here.'

'That would make five of us for dinner, then,' she mused. 'Though that turkey's easily big enough for twelve people.'

'Isn't it also traditional to have turkey as leftovers?' he asked.

'Well, yes,' she admitted.

'Then it will be fine for five. I'll invite Giacomo, Gina and her husband.'

'So it'll be like a family Christmas.'

She looked wistful, and Antonio realised what was missing. Family. He wasn't asking his family to meet her, not until she'd agreed to marry him; but he could invite hers to join them. 'Yes. I can fly your mother over. Give me ten minutes to arrange it. I'll sort out a private plane so she won't have to wait for a flight, and a car to take her to the airport in London and another one this end.'

Tia bit her lip. 'That's kind of you, but I think the journey might take it out of her too much.'

'Help me here, Tia,' he said softly. 'What do you want?'

'What you planned. That was a really nice thought.'

'But with more people, so it's like a real family Christmas?'

She nodded. 'And I want to help you prepare dinner. Even if you have got a gazillion alarms on your phone telling you what to do.' Her lips quirked. 'Mind you, I should've expected that. Nathan did stuff with military precision, too.'

'It works,' he said.

She grinned. 'So what now—you're going to cut every vegetable exactly the same length, and to make sure of it there's a tape measure next to your knife rack?'

There was a slight twinkle in her eye and Antonio couldn't help responding to it. 'Are you saying I need a tape measure?'

'Do you?' She lifted her chin.

Right then, she was near enough to kiss, and he almost, *almost* dipped his head to brush his mouth against hers. But then he could see the sudden panic in her eyes, as if the teasing had gone too far and had tipped into something else entirely, something she wasn't quite ready for.

This wasn't about putting pressure on her. It was about getting her to relax. About getting to know her. About letting her get to know him. So he pulled back. 'If we spend all this time talking about doing the veg instead of actually doing them,' he said, much more lightly than he felt, 'then our dinner guests are going to have to wait until tomorrow before we can feed them.'

'Good point,' she said.

'Let me call Gina and talk to Giacomo. And then we'll make dinner together.'

She really hadn't expected this. And she was seeing a completely different side to Antonio Valenti. He was trying to give her the family Christmas she missed so badly and longed for so much. And he wasn't standing on ceremony, insisting on asking the village's mayor and important personages to join them; he was perfectly happy to eat with her and his housekeeper and his security officer. He'd taken on board what she'd said about Christmas not being about money but about spending time together.

So, if she agreed to marry him and give the baby his name, maybe she wasn't going to be trapped in a completely loveless marriage. Maybe he was trying to show her that he could give her what she needed. That he could learn to love her and she could learn to love him.

Maybe, just maybe, this was going to work out.

Once Antonio had arranged for their dinner guests to join them, he brought out the vegetables, pans and sharp knives. 'OK. Crispy roast potatoes and parsnips, carrots, Brussels sprouts and red cabbage. I have chipolata sausages ready to be wrapped with bacon, and I have stuffing—which Gina says I should cook separately. What else?'

'That,' she said, 'is pretty comprehensive. Cranberry sauce?'

'Yes.' He grimaced. 'Though it's not homemade. It's in a jar.'

'A jar is fine. Gravy?'

'I think,' he said carefully, 'I might put you in charge of gravy.'

She smiled. 'So you're learning to delegate?'

He coughed. 'I believe your brother had a saying about pots and kettles.'

She laughed. 'OK. You have a point. I'm not very good at delegating, either.' But his mention of Nathan made her eyes prickle. 'I miss him. Nathan.'

'Me, too,' Antonio admitted.

'I was thinking. If our baby really is a boy, I'd like to call him Nathan—after my brother and my dad.' Though Nathan wasn't the only one Antonio had lost. 'And maybe his middle name could be Vincenzo, after your dad?'

'That,' Antonio said, 'would be perfect.'

Would the baby's last name be Valenti or Phillips? They still hadn't agreed on that bit. But this was a step in the right direction, she thought. They were starting to meet in the middle.

But Tia found herself enjoying the afternoon, preparing dinner together with Christmas music playing softly in the background. It really felt like the Christmases of her childhood, memories that pierced her heart with their sweetness.

Before their guests arrived, she showered and changed into the pretty dress Gina had bought for her.

'You look lovely,' Antonio said.

'Thank you.' So did he, in a formal white shirt, beautifully cut dark suit and understated silk tie. And his shoes were polished the same way as she remembered Nathan and her father polishing theirs, to a military mirror finish.

But could the Soldier Prince allow himself to be ruffled just enough at the edges to deal with a baby?

She pushed the thought aside. Not now. He'd gone to a lot of effort for her, and she wasn't going to start complaining.

Their guests arrived, and Antonio introduced Tia to Gina and her husband Enrico.

'It's lovely to meet you,' Tia said, hugging Gina. 'And thank you so much for finding me such beautiful clothes. It was so kind of you.'

'My pleasure, *piccola*,' Gina said, hugging her back.

Once their guests were seated, Tia helped Antonio bring in the first course, and then the dishes for the main. He carved the turkey at the table, just as she remembered her father doing when she was small, and they all helped themselves to the sides.

Tia was surprised to find how much she was

enjoying herself—and how relaxed Prince Antonio was.

Perhaps now was the right time to ask him…

'Do you have plans for tomorrow?' she asked.

'We can go exploring, if you like, take a drive deeper into the mountains,' he suggested.

'I have a better idea,' she said. 'When we were in the café this morning, I overheard someone talking about the village Christmas party for the children tomorrow afternoon.'

'They hold the party every year in the town hall,' Gina explained, 'for all the children in the villages who attend the *scuola elementary* and *asilo*—primary school and kindergarten. I used to help out, in the years when my Chiara and Matteo were young enough to go to the party.' Gina smiled. 'Basically the party's for children under the age of eleven, so there's dancing and games and party food and, of course, *Babbo Natale* to give each child a small gift.'

'Father Christmas,' Tia said. 'But the man who's supposed to be doing it this year can't do it now because he's just broken his leg skiing.'

Antonio looked puzzled. 'How do you know all this?'

'I overheard two of the organisers talking in

the ladies' yesterday. They said they couldn't find a replacement Father Christmas.' And this was the thing. Would the Prince think of his own child-to-be and unbend enough to do something kind for the children in the village— something that wouldn't cost him at all financially, but would mean giving up his time and doing something in person? 'And I was wondering,' she continued, 'if maybe you might offer to step in and help?'

'Me?' He looked as shocked as if she'd just suggested that he should take off all his clothes in public to raise money for charity.

He might put his life at risk, the way her brother had, for his job; but putting his dignity at risk was clearly a very different thing. A step too far, perhaps?

But she pressed on. 'All you'd have to do is put on a costume and a beard, maybe tie a pillow round your middle so you look plump enough to be Father Christmas, say, "Ho, ho, ho," a lot, and give each child a present.'

Dress up as *Babbo Natale*.

Antonio tried to get his head round it. This just wasn't the sort of thing his family did. And he hadn't had much to do with children, despite being the patron of a charity for children from an armed forces background who'd been bereaved; he had no idea how they would respond to him.

Then again, in three months' time he would have a baby of his own. He probably ought to take every opportunity he could to have some practice at being around babies and children.

Tia, he thought, would be a natural at being a mother. He could easily imagine her calming a fractious toddler in the coffee shop with a story or crayons, or soothing a baby while its tired mum sat down for two minutes with a cup of tea. And he could understand the attraction of the children's party for her, given that she'd had to put her dreams of being a primary school teacher to one side.

She wanted him to do this.

And it would be another step forward in his campaign to prove to her that they'd be good together and he would learn to be a good husband and father.

He took a deep breath. 'All right. I'll do it. Gina, given that you know about the party, do you know who's organising it?'

'Actually, I have the answer to that one,' Tia said. 'Excuse me for being rude and using tech at the table.' She grabbed her phone and pulled up a photograph. 'There was a poster in the café. The organiser's number is here.'

'Signora Capelli.' Although most of the villagers would speak English for the tourists, the children's Christmas party was for the locals, so the conversation had probably been in Italian. 'Do you speak much Italian, Tia?' he asked, curious.

She nodded. 'Giovanni and Vittoria—my bosses at the café—are originally from Naples. So over the years I've gradually learned from them.'

So even though she hadn't been able to travel, she'd at least had the pleasure of being able to learn another language.

He looked at her, then switched to Italian. 'If I play Father Christmas, will it make you happy?'

She paused for a bit, as if working out the correct phrases. '*Sì. Molto felice,*' she said.

He grinned. 'Then for you,' he said, switching back to English, 'I will do it. Giacomo, if I call and arrange it, would you…?'

'Sort out the security aspect? Of course,' his security officer said with a smile. 'Actually, sir, I think you would make a very good *Babbo Natale.*'

Antonio wasn't so sure, but he'd do it. 'Excuse me. As you said, Tia, tech at the table is rude, but let me make that call.'

A few minutes later, it was all arranged.

'They're delighted that I can help,' Antonio said. 'But I told them that you were the one who persuaded me to do it, so they'd like to invite you to come to the party as well.'

'I'd love to,' she said, and the sheer pleasure in her eyes made Antonio feel something odd in the region of his heart—as if something inside was cracking.

Once they'd eaten the fresh fruit and little Christmas fritters Antonio had prepared during the afternoon, he ushered everyone through to the sitting room.

'But surely we need to clear up first?' Tia asked.

'No. I'll sort it out later. Tonight is for having fun,' he said. 'Let's go through to the sitting room.'

They played a few rounds of charades, half in

English and half in Italian. And then Antonio brought out a box that he'd had delivered earlier that day, containing a copy of the musical game with kazoos that Tia had told him about enjoying so much.

Tears glittered in her eyes as he placed the box on the table.

He went to stand next to her. 'I ordered it online for delivery today. Did I do the wrong thing?' he asked softly, taking her hand. 'Because we don't have to play the game if you'd rather not. I apologise for upsetting you. That wasn't my intention.'

'No, it's a really kind thought.' She swallowed hard. 'I have such lovely memories of playing this with Mum and Dad and Nathan. And now I'm going to have lovely memories of playing with you.'

He didn't want this to be just a memory. He wanted it to be the start of a whole new tradition. But he didn't know how to tell her. Instead, awkwardly, he squeezed her hand.

Several times during the game, Tia caught his eye and his heart felt as if it had done a backflip. And several times he could see the baby kicking. It blew him away. He'd never expected to feel anything like this, and he really wasn't sure how to deal with it. All he could do was be the polite, perfect host, the way he'd been brought up to be. And he wished he could let himself go as easily as Tia, Gina, Giacomo and Enrico seemed to be able to do. But nobody in his family ever let go like that. He'd just have to try harder.

Or maybe that was the point: this should be effortless, and he was trying too hard. And the crack he'd felt inside him earlier seemed to freeze up again.

'Time to make some tea,' Tia said, holding her sides. 'I need a break from laughing.'

'I'll help you,' Gina said. She followed Tia into the kitchen and stacked the dishwasher while Tia filled the kettle and put cups and a teapot on a tray. She winked at the younger woman. 'I know the Prince said he'd clear up tomorrow, but men never stack the dishwasher properly.'

'That's what Vittoria says about Giovanni at work,' Tia said with a smile. Gina reminded her very much of her boss, making her feel completely relaxed and at home.

'I've known Prince Antonio for many years, since he was tiny and his family first came here to this house,' Gina said. 'But this is the first time I've seen him look this relaxed, as an adult. It's not my place to ask questions, but…?' She looked pointedly at Tia's bump.

Tia knew the older woman had Antonio's best interests at heart. 'Yes, the baby is his.' She wrinkled her nose. 'But it's complicated.'

'Antonio needs love in his life,' Gina said softly. 'King Vincenzo was always very formal with both the boys. Queen Maria was a bit less so, but there was still always a little reserve and they never really had a proper childhood, even here. I think you and the baby might be good for Prince Antonio.' She flapped a hand. 'But I'm speaking out of turn.'

'Not at all,' Tia reassured her. 'And I won't say a word of what you said to the Prince.'

It hadn't occurred to her before that maybe the Prince didn't have everything in his life— that maybe her love and the baby would be a gift to him. But, the more she thought about it, the more she realised that he really was the 'poor little rich boy' and their positions were completely reversed. Although she was financially and socially much poorer than him, when it came to love and family she was so much richer.

But would she and the baby be enough for him?

Because, even though she felt she'd grown so much closer to Antonio today—that she was more than halfway to falling in love with the man behind the royal mask—she didn't think he felt the same about her. Antonio was all about duty, and she wasn't sure that she could live a life without love. If he married her purely because he thought it was the right thing to do, could he grow to love her and the baby? And did she really want to live in a world where everything they did or said was put under the microscope of public opinion?

She forced the thought away and took the tray of tea through, smiling at Antonio, Giacomo and Enrico. But her busy day started to catch up with her, and she found herself yawning.

'I'm so sorry,' she said. 'I don't mean to be rude.'

'Being pregnant is tiring, child,' Gina said. 'Go to bed. We understand.'

'Thank you. And thank you all for such a

lovely evening. It really felt like a proper Christmas,' she said.

But by the time she climbed into bed, she was wide awake and worrying again.

Antonio had been very quiet after dinner. Was he having second thoughts about this? Could he grow to love her? Should she marry him, give the baby his protection? Or would she be better off going back to London and bringing up their baby in love and relative obscurity?

CHAPTER FIVE

ANTONIO HAD ALMOST finished clearing up in the kitchen when his phone pinged.

Who would message him this late at night? It must be something important, he thought, and picked up his phone to see a message from Luca.

I thought you should know about this before it hits the media tomorrow.

There was an attachment to the message: a PDF of a press release.

Antonio read it and blew out a breath. According to the press release, the DNA test proved beyond all doubt that Gabriella was the oldest child of King Vincenzo, and the palace would like to announce that she would accede to the throne rather than Luca. Luca would remain in his role as the Crown Prince and would

202 SOLDIER PRINCE'S SECRET BABY GIFT

support his older sister through the beginning of her reign.

As soon as this news reached the media, Antonio realised, it would be splashed over the front pages of the newspapers. And he would be expected back at the palace as soon as possible. Which meant time was running out for his impromptu getaway with Tia.

His duty meant that he ought to fly back first thing in the morning. Or even tonight.

But he'd promised to play *Babbo Natale* at the village children's Christmas party.

Although he knew the organisers would understand him having to duck out at the last minute, given the news, it would mean leaving them in a mess. And Antonio Valenti was a man who kept his promises. He didn't want to disappoint the children or the villagers—and he really didn't want to disappoint Tia.

But if he didn't go back to the palace first thing tomorrow, he would disappoint his family.

Whatever he did, he was going to let someone down.

Thinking about it logically, he knew that his

brother, his mother and Gabriella had each other and all the resources of the palace to support them. Tia had nobody; although she would have emotional support from her mother, Grace Phillips wasn't well enough to deal with the inevitable media intrusion. The stress might even bring on a relapse of her medical condition.

Well, he wasn't going to abandon Tia for a third time.

He typed a message into his phone.

Thanks for update. Will be back in a couple of days. Things I need to do here first.

He was surprised when a message came back almost immediately.

Miles told me who Tia was, but he refused to tell me anything else. Though someone in the office told me she looks very pregnant. Assume congratulations are in order?

Oh. With Tia being so petite, her bump really showed. Of course people would gossip in the palace, even if Miles told them not to, about the pregnant woman who'd come to see the Prince, and Antonio's subsequent disappearance. He'd be naive to think otherwise.

Does Mamma know?

I haven't said anything. I think this needs to come from you.

Of course it did. He already knew that.

Hopefully the media will concentrate on events here. Wrap things up and come back as soon as you can.

Thanks. I will.

Antonio was pretty sure that Luca would leave it at that, but then his phone pinged again.

So do you have a view of snow?

Of course his brother would guess where he'd gone. Antonio had been fooling himself to think otherwise. Picco Innevato was where Antonio always went when he needed some space after a difficult mission.

Yes.

Christmassy. That's nice.

Antonio nearly typed back, *Who are you and what have you done with my older brother?* But, actually, it was nice to feel that for once his older brother wasn't as unbending as their father.

Yes, it is. I put a tree up in the house.

Though he wasn't entirely sure that Luca would understand about him playing *Babbo Natale* at the children's Christmas party. Not when a major announcement was being made and he really ought to be back at the palace, supporting his family.

I'll message you when I'm on my way back.

Good luck. I hope it works out with Tia. Finding someone who loves you—that's special.

And then the penny finally dropped.

Luca had changed. When he'd come back from meeting Gabriella at Crystal Lake, he'd been different. And Antonio was pretty sure that it had a lot to do with Imogen Albright,

the woman he'd met out there and become engaged to.

His brother was in love; and that love had
melted his habitual reserve.

Antonio couldn't quite get his head round the
fact that his elder brother was actually wishing
him luck in love.

Then again, he knew he needed luck. If he
couldn't persuade Tia to love him, he needed at
the very least a good working relationship with
the mother of his baby—a child who was definitely going to be fourth in line to the throne.

Me, too, he typed, though this time he didn't
send the message.

The next morning, Antonio checked the main
news sites on his phone. They were full of the
shock announcement about Gabriella, the long-
lost Princess of Casavalle who was about to become the new Queen. And quite a few of them
seemed to have noticed that Prince Antonio
wasn't at the palace and were asking exactly
where he was.

Thankfully the villagers at Picco Innevato
had always been protective of his family, and
he knew that none of them would sell him out

to the media. Until he'd persuaded Tia to marry him and let him give her and the baby his protection, he wanted to stay well out of the limelight.

Today was their last full day in the village in any case, but he knew that time was running out. He needed to wrap things up here and go back to the palace.

He sent a holding message to his mother, Gabriella and Miles—all of whom had texted him that morning—saying that he'd be back tomorrow but had some things he needed to do first. He knew the message was vague, and it would no doubt infuriate them all, but he'd learned in the army that you needed to do the right things in the right order. Tia had to come first.

When she came downstairs, he made her breakfast. Now wasn't the time to worry her about palace politics. He wanted to concentrate on *her*. 'I was going to ask your advice.'

'My advice?' She looked surprised. 'About what?'

'The children's party. It's a little outside my usual sphere.' Which was an understatement. 'I've rarely had contact with children with my family duties, even as patron of the charity—I tend to work with the fundraisers rather than the children.'

'And you don't know what to do?'

'No,' he admitted. 'I'm guessing that your customers at the café include families with children.' Plus he knew she'd dreamed of being a primary school teacher. So she must have some idea of how to work with children.

'Just be yourself,' she said. 'After you've finished being *Babbo Natale*—and obviously make sure that none of them see you change out of the costume—I think just join in with the games.'

Could it really be that simple? 'OK.' But then there was the party. 'Maybe I ought to do more for the party. Perhaps I could pay for the presents?'

'Christmas really isn't about money and heaps of expensive presents,' she said softly, 'it's about spending time with people and making them feel good. When you were a child—I know things were a bit different for you, but wasn't the best part of Christmas playing games with your brother?'

He thought about it.

Just as last night hadn't been about presents—it had been about having fun, and that one game he'd bought had meant more to Tia than if he'd bought her the richest and most exclusive of jewels.

'Yes.'

'Well, then,' she said. 'And I'm sure the organisers have already sorted everything out. If you go in and say you're going to buy extra presents for the children, it's kind of like you telling them that whatever they've already done isn't good enough.'

'I hadn't really thought about it in that way.' He looked awkwardly at her. 'Just that with my family's background, I feel I ought to do more.'

'Time's so much more important than money. Anyone can buy gifts; it's the easy way out,' she said. 'And not just anyone's prepared to dress up as Santa and be patient with children who are shy or nervous. The people in the village will appreciate what you're doing so much more than if you call a shop and pay for a huge sackful of presents to be wrapped. You're giving something of *yourself*. What the children want at the Christmas party is Father Christmas. And today that's going to be you.'

Tia Phillips looked like an ordinary woman.

But Antonio was beginning to learn just how extraordinary she was.

'You're right,' he said. 'They want Father Christmas.'

He knew he really ought to tell her about what was going on in the palace, especially as it meant that they'd have to leave Picco Innevato tomorrow, but he knew she was looking forward to the party and he didn't want to spoil today for her. There was time enough for them to have to deal with the politics. He'd tell her tomorrow.

Half an hour before the party was due to start, he and Tia went into the village hall to meet the organisers.

'We're so grateful, Your Royal Highness,' Signora Capelli said.

'It's nice to be able to do something for the village,' Antonio said. 'So what exactly do I do?'

'Once in costume, *Babbo Natale* sits on the chair in the grotto,' Signora Capelli said, indicating the chair festooned with tinsel underneath an arch decorated with more tinsel and cut-out Christmas trees that had clearly been painted by the children. 'He greets each child, wishes them a merry Christmas and gives them a present.'

He could do that.

'We've put the presents into sacks, split by age group, and your helper will tell you the name and the age of each child just before they come to see you,' Signora Capelli continued.

'Thank you,' Antonio said. 'That's very clear. Who's my helper?' He looked at Tia. Given that he was dressing up as Father Christmas, would she be prepared to dress up as an elf?

Signora Capelli smiled. 'I would suggest Tia, but her condition is a little...distinctive.'

Her baby bump. Of course the children would notice that the guest at their party had the same bump as *Babbo Natale*'s helper.

'But perhaps you'd like to help us with the table, Tia?' Signora Capelli asked.

'Of course,' Tia said with a smile. She indicated the other helpers, who were wearing Santa hats or reindeer antlers. 'And I'm perfectly happy to wear a hat or reindeer antlers if you want me to.'

'Antlers. Of course.' Signora Capelli looked anxious. 'Sir, forgive me for being rude, but

I assume you know the names of all the reindeer?'

'Rudolph,' he said. Then he stopped. He didn't actually know any others. It wasn't something they'd ever talked about at the palace or in the army.

Tia laughed. 'Don't worry—I do. Dasher and Dancer, Prancer and Vixen, Comet and Cupid, Donner and Blitzen.' She made him repeat the names until he was word-perfect, and it made him realise what a fabulous teacher she'd make.

He changed into the costume and beard. 'You're right. I need padding,' he said.

Signora Capelli found some cushions and Tia, wearing antlers and looking incredibly cute with her huge brown eyes and curly black hair, helped him put the final touches to his outfit.

Tia stood back with her hands on her hips and looked at him. 'Perfect.'

Never in a million years would he have expected to do something like this. Or that she'd have tears in her eyes.

'Are you all right?' he asked.

'Yes. It's just… Thank you for doing this, Antonio. For making things right for the children.' Impulsively, she hugged him; and the feeling of something cracking in the middle of his chest intensified.

As soon as he was sitting on the tinsel 'throne' in his grotto—a million miles away from the real throne in their palace—the children streamed into the hall and a queue formed to meet him. He didn't have time to watch out for Tia, because he was too busy playing his role, and he found himself improvising when a child asked him about the North Pole and what the elves did there.

'They help me make gifts and wrap them up for the children who would like them,' he said, crossing his fingers mentally.

Another child asked him about the reindeer, and he was grateful that Tia had drilled him on the right names.

Every single child seemed thrilled with their gift from *Babbo Natale*, but it didn't take long for Antonio to realise that Tia had been right when she'd said that Christmas wasn't about the presents: today was all about the gifts of time and love and kindness.

The smiles on their faces warmed his heart. Then one little boy gave him a carrot. 'It's a present for Rudolph,' he said.

'Thank you very much,' Antonio said. 'Carrots are his favourite. He'll be delighted to share that with his friends for dinner.'

Another little girl who must've been about seven shyly handed him a Cellophane wrapper tied with a bow. 'You always bring us presents every year, *Babbo Natale*,' she said, 'but nobody brings you one and I think they should. My *mamma* helped me make this for you this morning and I put special sprinkles on it and I wrapped it just for you.'

There was a huge lump in his throat. A small, thoughtful gift that felt incredibly special. Over the years, as a child, he'd been given incredibly expensive and exclusive gifts; but this one was *personal*. One that taught him the real meaning of Christmas. 'That's so kind of you,' he said. 'It looks so pretty. I'll enjoy that with my glass of milk later today. Thank you so much.'

When he'd given the last child their present, he waved goodbye to everyone and wished everyone a merry Christmas, then headed out of the hall back to the room where he'd changed into the costume. He folded everything up neatly—Tia would no doubt tease him about doing it with military precision, just as she'd teased him about his schedule for cooking Christmas dinner—and then headed back towards the hall.

Tia was waiting for him just outside. 'Are you OK?' she asked.

'Yes. That was amazing—really humbling.' He blew out a breath and nodded through the open doorway. 'See that little girl over there with the curly black hair in the blue dress?'

'Yes.'

'She gave me a cookie, all prettily wrapped. She'd made it especially for me this morning with her mother's help and chose the sprinkles. She said nobody ever brings *Babbo Natale* a present and she...' Suddenly, he just couldn't say anything else.

She hugged him, clearly realising how deeply the gift had affected him. 'That's what Christmas is about,' she said. 'It's the thought behind the gift, how personal it is.'

Right then, he knew exactly what he wanted for Christmas.

Tia.

And their baby.

But he didn't know how to tell her. He couldn't get the words out. They stuck in his throat. But he wanted her so much. Needed her. Needed both of them.

Why was it so hard to say it? Why couldn't he just open his mouth and say, 'Tia, the way I feel about you puts my head in a spin and I can't find the right words, but please stay with me'?

This wasn't the place, either. And it was too important for him to mess up by simply blurting out the jumble in his head.

'We'd better get back to the party,' she said.

The children insisted that the Prince and Tia should share their party tea—bruschetta, cherry tomatoes, carrot sticks, little cubes of cheese and ham and the traditional Italian *tronchetti di Natale*.

'I love chocolate Yule log,' Tia said with a smile, accepting a slice.

Both he and Tia danced with the children and joined in the games—sticking a carrot 'nose' on the outline of a snowman while their eyes were covered with a scarf, guessing the items in a stocking just by feeling them, using a paper straw to blow a cotton wool 'snowball' in a race to the finish line, and 'Christmas ornament' musical chairs, where the children danced round the cut-out ornaments as the

music played and had to stand on an ornament
when the music stopped.

It was way, way outside anything Antonio
had ever done before, though he suspected from
the way that Tia joined in that she'd maybe
been involved with something similar at the
café where she worked. And he was surprised
by how much fun it was, everything from the
games to the dancing. It made him feel different—part of the village, more so than he did
even as a child, and he really felt connected
with his people.

He realised then that the weird feeling in his
chest was happiness. Here in Picco Innevato at
the children's party, he felt accepted for who he
was, instead of being seen as a remote prince.
He'd never even had that feeling in the army,
where he had previously been at his happiest.

So much for persuading Tia; what he'd actually done was persuade himself. Because Tia
had shown him how good life could be, how it
felt to be part of a family—and that was what
he wanted. To see her eyes sparkle and her
face glow with happiness as she danced with
the children, to see her glance over at him and
smile with a warmth that made his own heart

sing. He wanted to see her look like that while she danced with their own child in the middle of their kitchen. A private moment far from the formality of his day-to-day life.

Once the party was over, he and Tia helped to clear up, hugged all the organisers good-bye, and walked back through the village to his house.

'I believe you now about doing your fair share of the cleaning,' she said with a smile. 'Seeing you wielding that broom with military pr—'

'Tia,' he cut in, 'that particular joke is wearing just a little bit thin.'

'But it was,' she said, her smile broadening into a grin. 'Watching you sweep a floor was like watching a man with a mower making a stripy lawn.'

He thought about kissing her to stop her talking.

But that was too tempting—and too danger-ous to his peace of mind. If he let himself give in to his feelings, if he said the wrong thing and scared her away... Plus they were in a pub-lic place. He'd wait until they were back at the house. And maybe the walk home would give him enough time to put his thoughts and his feelings back in order. Instead, he said, 'The Christmas market in the square looks really pretty, all lit up for night-time.'

Thankfully it distracted her, and she smiled at him. 'That'd be nice.'

And when she allowed him to take her arm— which was ostensibly for safety in case she slipped, but was really because he just wanted to be close to her—he was shocked to discover that it made him feel as if he'd just conquered the world.

'We have a Christmas market a bit like this on the South Bank in London,' she said. 'You can buy mulled wine, hot chocolate, various foods and gifts. And then you can cross the river over to Somerset House and go to the skating rink. But here it's different—the hot chocolate is much thicker, and there are those gorgeous nativity scenes everywhere.'

When they got to the stalls, she stopped by the little wooden shack offering snow globes for sale, and her eye seemed to be caught by one in particular—a crystalline star suspended inside the globe and set on a crystal base. She picked it up, and her dark eyes gleamed with pleasure.

But then she examined the base, looked regretful and replaced it carefully.

Antonio had the strongest feeling that she loved the globe, but she'd just seen the price and it was outside her budget. He knew that Tia would be too proud to admit that she couldn't afford it, and if he insisted on buying it for her right now she'd be embarrassed and awkward. But there was a way around it: he'd buy it without her knowing and give it to her later, in private. A surprise gift. And he'd make it clear there were no strings. He stood behind her so she couldn't see his face, caught the stall-holder's eye and mimed to him to save the snow globe for him. The stall-holder glanced at Tia, clearly checking to make sure she couldn't see his reaction and guess what was going on, then winked at Antonio.

At the next stall, when Tia bought a scented candle decorated with pressed flowers for her mother, Antonio excused himself and went back to get the snow globe she'd liked. The stall-holder wrapped it in a box tied with a bright scarlet ribbon; Antonio slipped the box into his pocket so it wasn't visible. He'd give it to Tia later, when the time was right.

* * *

Antonio insisted on carrying Tia's purchase from the candle stall but, when he went to tuck her hand into his arm for balance, somehow they ended up holding hands.

At the party, Tia had seen a whole new side to the Prince.

Sure, he'd been a bit formal and over the top when he'd helped clear up, marching up and down with the broom as if he was on a military parade: but he *had* helped, as if he was just another one of the villagers and not the man who was third in line to the throne of Casavalle. And the way he'd been with the children… Even though she knew he'd had such a formal upbringing and he'd actually asked her advice about what to do at the party, he'd then done his best to fit in and make the afternoon fun for the children. She'd taken a sneaky snap of him on her phone while he'd been playing the snowball-blowing game, surrounded by children and laughing, and he'd really looked as if he belonged.

It gave her so much hope for the future. From what she'd seen, she really believed that Antonio could learn to be a warm, loving father.

That maybe he could escape his upbringing and learn to be *himself.* And that maybe she was the one who could help him do that. To think that she might be the one to finally unlock his heart was amazing: it would be a real privilege, even though it scared her because she might not be up to the task. Though, for the sake of their baby—and for themselves—she'd make sure she was good enough.

As they walked up the steps to the porch leading to his front door, he paused.

'What?' she asked.

'What do you see?' he asked.

'Your front door. A Christmas wreath.' The one with copper-painted honesty seed pods that they'd bought together. 'Gorgeous sparkly lights on the trees on either side of the door.' Immaculately clipped cones of yew that were no doubt measured to get them that precise shape.

'And?' He glanced upwards, indicating where she should look.

'Mistletoe.' She caught her breath. Was he suggesting they should...? 'Do you have a tradition about mistletoe in Italy?' she asked, her voice hoarse.

He inclined his head. 'Here it tends to be New Year's Eve when you kiss under the mistletoe. But you're English, so I think perhaps we should use the English tradition.'

Which meant kissing under the mistletoe at Christmas...

Then again, they'd decorated the house for Christmas and he'd cooked them a proper Christmas dinner. This was a sort of early Christmas. It counted.

So she made no protest when he dipped his head and kissed her, his mouth warm and sweet and coaxing. She leaned into the kiss and slid her hands into his hair, drawing him closer. He wrapped his arms round her, holding her tightly, and kissed her until she was dizzy.

There was suddenly a volley of kicks in her stomach, and he broke the kiss, laughing. 'I think someone wants to tell us something.'

'That might be the baby equivalent of saying "Get a room",' she said ruefully.

He rested his hand on her bump. 'This blows my mind. Our baby.'

The expression on his face was a mixture of pride and tenderness and... No, Tia didn't dare let herself hope for anything else. But if he bonded with their baby, that would be a good thing—both for Antonio and for their baby.

She shivered, and he brushed his mouth against hers again. 'Sorry. I shouldn't keep you on the doorstep in the cold.' He unlocked the front door and ushered her inside.

Right at that moment it felt as if they were a proper couple. As if they were just coming home from an event in the village—leaving their coats on the bentwood stand in the hallway and ending up in the kitchen, where he put the kettle on while she got the mugs out.

'So did you enjoy the party?' she asked.

'More than I expected to,' he said.

She showed him the picture she'd taken on the phone. 'You looked as if you were having fun.'

'Something so simple. I never did things like that as a child,' he said. 'But our baby definitely will.'

And Tia felt as if her world had just exploded into colour.

'So, we have leftovers for dinner.' He smiled

at her. 'What sort of thing did you do as a child?'

'Cold turkey, home-made chips or French bread, and salad,' she said promptly. 'And Mum used to make vegetable and turkey soup. We used to wrap up warm and go to the beach, the day after Boxing Day, and we'd take a flask of Mum's soup and have a picnic.'

He wrapped his arms round her. 'I know it won't be the same, but we have beaches here. I'd be happy to take you.'

Which sounded as if he saw a future for them.

Even though part of her wanted to be sensible and acknowledge that their lives were too far apart for them to be together, part of her was thrilled by the idea. Warmed by hope that maybe he wanted a future for them—and Antonio Valenti was the kind of man who'd make things happen. If he wanted her, really wanted her in his life, then he'd find a way through the traditions that bound him.

And she'd meet him halfway.

In the end, they made turkey salad sandwiches and ate them in the kitchen, then went into the conservatory to curl up on a sofa together and watch the stars and talk about anything and everything.

Tia was so easy to be with.

Antonio wished it could always be like this, but he knew they'd have to go back to the palace soon and face real life, the politics and the press. Eventually she fell asleep and he sat there just holding her.

He knew now that this was what he wanted: to be a family with her and their baby, to live out of the limelight of the palace and be part of the community of the village. He wanted her to be his wife, his partner in everything.

But he couldn't work out how to tell her. If he asked her to marry him now, would she believe him that he wanted her for herself, or would she still think he was asking her purely out of a sense of duty and honour?

'I want to be a family with you,' he whispered.

She didn't wake, so he gently eased her out of his arms, then fetched a blanket and tucked it round her. She looked so cute, curled up on the sofa. And so *right*. He resisted the temptation to kiss her awake, because there was something else he needed to do. A letter that he should've written a long time ago.

He fetched notepaper, an envelope and a pen from his office—an impersonal typed letter was absolutely not good enough for this—and took a photograph from his wallet. And then he began to write.

When he'd finished, Tia was still asleep.

He knelt by her and stroked her cheek. 'Tia? Tia, wake up, *bella*,' he whispered.

She opened her eyes, looking lost and incredibly vulnerable.

'Time to go to bed,' he said, and gently helped her to her feet.

'Sorry. I didn't mean to fall asleep on you.' She bit her lip, looking guilty.

'You're six months pregnant and you've had a busy day. I think you're allowed to fall asleep,' he said, smiling.

He was so tempted to carry her up the stairs, though he knew that wouldn't be fair. But at the door to her room he couldn't resist kissing her goodnight.

Her eyes were huge as she stroked his face. 'Antonio.'

He kissed her again.

'Stay with me tonight?' she asked.

Fall asleep with her in his arms. Wake up with her in his arms.

How could he possibly resist?

And this time he did pick her up and carry her to bed.

Afterwards, it took him a long time to fall asleep, because he knew now that this was what he wanted more than anything else. To be with her. And for her to want to be with him.

Please let her want the same thing.

Please.

Later that night, Tia woke when the baby started somersaulting. Antonio's arms were wrapped round her, and she felt safe and warm and cherished.

Could this work out, or was it just a hopeless fantasy?

She and Antonio had come so far over the last couple of days; but she had no idea whether his family would accept her. She knew that her father's family had rejected her mother, and she knew how much the situation had hurt both her parents. What if this turned out to be the same sort of thing?

Then, whatever she did, she lost. She didn't want to make Antonio choose between his family and her, because that wasn't fair; yet leaving him and quietly taking the baby away to live anonymously in London was no longer an option. Not now she'd seen the joy in his eyes when he'd felt their baby kick inside her.

Please, please let this work out…

CHAPTER SIX

THE NEXT MORNING, Tia was woken by the sound of a phone shrilling. At first she was disoriented but then last night came rushing back to her. How she'd fallen asleep on the sofa in Antonio's arms. How he'd ushered her up to bed, and she'd asked him to stay. How tenderly he'd held her…

The shrilling was from Antonio's phone, and he was sitting up in bed, frowning and speaking rapidly in Italian.

He was speaking too quickly for her to follow what he was saying, but something was clearly wrong, because he ended the call and then appeared to be looking up something on his phone.

She sat up. 'What is it?'

'Ah, Tia. Good morning.'

'What's happened?'

He grimaced. 'That was Gina on the phone.

Apparently the media have descended on the village. There's some stuff in the news.'

'What stuff?'

He handed her the phone in silence.

It was a newsfeed showing the front pages of various newspapers and headlines for their stories. Someone had clearly taken photographs last night when Antonio had kissed her on the doorstep.

One of the pages had mocked up a kind of photo love story: in the first photograph he was kissing her, the second had her sliding her arms round his neck and kissing him back, and the third showed her smiling at him while he rested his hand on her bump, obviously feeling the baby kick.

The first one was captioned *Who's that girl?* The second bore the line *A kiss is just a kiss— or is it?* The third had a heart drawn round them and was captioned *Baby Love?*

She read through the actual article. It was asking who she was, and if this was Prince Antonio's secret baby.

Is this the third baby scandal to rock the kingdom of Casavalle in recent months?

The oldest child of King Vincenzo, Gabriella, was kept secret for decades, Prince Luca's fiancée was pregnant with someone else's baby, and now it seems Vincenzo's youngest child isn't to be left out of the scandal...

Horrified, Tia realised that the story was going to cause huge waves in Casavalle and also in London. If the media started digging to find out who she was, then her mother was going to be dragged into this.

She skimmed over the speculation, and then came to the last paragraph.

Prince Luca has confirmed that his older half-sister Gabriella will be acceding to the throne instead of him, with the coronation due at the end of the year.

So Gabriella was definitely becoming Queen? Since when? Antonio hadn't mentioned anything about that to her. He'd said that they were waiting for DNA test results and Gabriella's decision. 'Gabriella's actually becoming Queen?' she asked.

'With the support of our family, yes,' he said.

She frowned. 'Did you know about this?'

'Yes. Luca sent me the press release.'

Her stomach felt tied in knots as she took in the coolness of his expression and his tone. She'd been so sure that he was thawing out. But now he'd gone all aloof on her again. He was reverting to being Antonio the Prince, and she realised that she had just been kidding herself. Antonio was a prince first and foremost. Even if he did thaw out with her again, it would never be for long.

'You didn't say anything to me.' The words came out before she could stop them. How stupid of her. Why would he feel he needed to tell her anything about Palace business?

And then a really nasty thought sneaked into her head.

If he'd known about the press release, known that the press would be asking about him... Suddenly his actions of yesterday took on a whole new meaning. 'So you must've known the media would want to know where you were, when it was obvious you weren't at the palace.'

'I didn't think they'd find me here,' he said.

How, when it was his family's house so it was an obvious place to look? 'But they did—

and they took that photograph.' She swallowed hard. 'On your doorstep.'

'I didn't notice any flash.'

Neither had she. She didn't *think* he was lying. But she did feel manipulated, and she wasn't sure whether she was more angry with herself for not realising that of course he was a prince and the media would follow him relentlessly, or with him for bringing her here in the first place and not letting her go quietly back to London where nobody would know about her or the baby.

The phone shrilled again, and the palace secretary's name flashed up on the caller ID.

'For you,' she said, handing the phone back to him.

She couldn't hear what Miles was saying, and she could tell nothing at all from Antonio's side of the conversation. His face was completely impassive, and all he seemed to say was 'Yes', 'No' or 'I see'.

He ended the call and looked at her. 'Miles says the media knows who you are, that you live in London and you're a waitress.'

She looked at him in dismay. 'Does that mean they're going to go after my mum now?' And maybe her bosses. Her friends. Anyone who'd known her even vaguely in the last twenty years. The media wouldn't care, as long as they got their story.

'It's a strong possibility,' he admitted. 'I'm sorry you've been dragged into this.'

'Are you?' she asked, with the doubts still nagging at her. 'Or did you engineer it, knowing that you're the only one who could protect my mum so I'd have to agree to all your demands?'

He stared at her, saying nothing, and with a sick feeling she realised she hadn't just been hormonal and paranoid. This really was manipulation. She'd been fooling herself yesterday, thinking that he was getting closer to her and hoping that maybe, after all, this was going to work out. He didn't love her, but she was carrying his heir, the fourth in line to the throne, so he thought it was his duty to give the baby his name. She'd already refused to marry him, so he'd put her in a situation where she'd *have* to agree.

The cold, unemotional soldier was a master strategist.

He knew that Tia would do anything to protect her mother. If her mother was in danger from being hounded by the media, then Tia would agree to anything to stop that.

So he'd got close to her. Made her think that he cared. Put her in the perfect position for a photo opportunity.

And now...

This time her mobile phone was the one to ring.

Seeing their neighbour's name on the screen made her heart freeze for a second.

Was Becky ringing to tell her that her mother was ill—or worse? Please, no. She couldn't lose her last family member. Please. *Please.*

'Hello, Becky,' she said, trying to keep the panic from her voice. 'Is Mum all right?'

'Yes, love, she's fine. Don't worry,' her neighbour reassured her.

Which was when she started shivering, in reaction to the fear that had flooded through her.

Antonio moved to put his arm round her, but she didn't believe it was to warm her or comfort her. This was all about duty and control, and she'd been too stupid to see it.

She angled herself away from him, and thankfully he took the hint and backed off.

'But there's reporters and photographers everywhere,' Becky said. 'I went out to get a pint of milk and everyone kept asking me about you. I just told them you were a lovely girl and to leave you alone.'

'Thank you. I really appreciate that.' With neighbours like Becky on their side, at least Tia knew that her mother was going to be OK. She took a deep breath. 'I'll be home as soon as I can. I'll text you when I know the flight times. And I'll ring Mum in a second.'

'All right, love. Don't you worry. I'll keep an eye on her.' Becky paused. 'Your young man's very handsome.'

He wasn't exactly hers, though like a fool she'd let herself start to believe that he might be. And wasn't the old saying, 'Handsome is as handsome does'? But Becky was waiting for an answer. She didn't need to know what a mess this was. 'Yes,' Tia said. 'I'll see you soon. And thank you again.'

'Is your mother all right?' Antonio asked as soon as she ended the call.

No thanks to him. 'Yes,' she said, her voice cool. 'Don't worry. You win. I'll do what you want and marry you so you get your heir—but only on condition you take care of my mum and make sure the media doesn't hassle her.'

At least he didn't look full of triumph.

Then again, he wasn't showing any emotion at all.

How, just how, had her brother been friends with him? Or was he totally different at work?

Not that it mattered.

Nothing mattered any more.

She'd been very naive to think he was starting to care for her. Antonio the Automaton. He'd just been a very, very shrewd tactician.

Military precision.

How stupid she'd been to tease him about that. It was exactly what it had been. Who he was.

'I'll arrange for someone to handle things for your mother in London,' Antonio said. 'Although I think it would be best to fly her to Casavalle.'

'So she gets no say in it, either? Like the baby, she's going to be another royal pawn in a game?' she asked bitterly.

'Tia, it isn't like that.'

'Isn't it?' She looked levelly at him. 'If you'll excuse me, I'd like to shower and get dressed.'

In clothes he'd arranged for her, because she'd been so carried away with the gorgeous Christmas he'd made for her that she hadn't done any laundry. Leaving her with no choice. Just as the rest of her life was going to be now.

Stupid, stupid, stupid.

Right at that second, she felt *bought*.

Tia had already made up her mind, so there was no point in arguing with her, Antonio thought. Right now it would only make matters worse. And if he upset her, it would be bad for the baby. He needed her to be calm. Maybe, if he didn't escalate things, when she'd had time to think logically about it she'd realise that he hadn't been trying to manipulate her. That he'd been caught unawares, too.

Instead, he said neutrally, 'I'll arrange for a flight back to the palace.'

'Thank you.'

'And for you to go back to London. Please call your mother and reassure her that I'll do everything in my power to protect her.'

'Of course, Your Royal Highness.'

That hurt. That she could be so formal with

him after what they'd shared. That she could believe he'd engineered this whole thing.

Thankfully his upbringing meant that the hurt didn't show.

And he'd do this logically. Get the media spotlight off them, and then once they were in the palace he could start to sort things out with her.

'I'll leave a suitcase outside your door,' he said.

'Suitcase?' She looked surprised.

'For your clothes.' When it looked as if she was about to argue, he raked a hand through his hair. 'Tia. There were no strings to those clothes.'

'I suppose you can't have your bride-to-be wearing cheap chainstore clothes in public,' she said.

Did she really think he was such a snob, that he gave a damn about money? The unfairness stung enough for him to say, 'Don't be so ridiculous.'

'Ridiculous?'

'I'm not a snob. It's nothing to do with money. I was trying to do something nice for you without rubbing your nose in the difference between our financial situations or making you feel be-holden to me.'

She looked crestfallen then, and he felt guilty—because by saying that out loud he'd done precisely what he'd been trying not to do. He'd rubbed her nose in it. She'd been angry and hurt and snapping at him, but he shouldn't have snapped back and continued the fight. Time to back off. Not because he was in the wrong or afraid of a fight, but because she was out of sorts and he needed to think of the baby. 'I'm going to have a shower and go downstairs. I'll make breakfast when you're ready.'

She nodded, and looked away.

He left her room, showered and dressed swiftly, and sent holding texts to his brother, his mother and Gabriella, saying that he'd ex-plain everything when he was back at the pal-ace later that morning. He took the special glass bauble from the tree and wrapped it up, then added an addendum to the letter he'd written the previous night, and stowed them both in his bag along with the wrapped snow globe.

Tia was silent when she finally came down-stairs. For a moment, he thought she was going to refuse breakfast. So he just said quietly, 'You need to eat. For you and the baby.'

There was a movement across her stomach. At least the baby agreed with him, he thought wryly.

She shrugged, still looking hurt and angry, but at least she ate her toast. Drank the mug of tea he'd prepared. Climbed into the back of the car—this time, Giacomo drove, and the windows were blacked out to avoid the press.

Tia stared out of the window all the way to the airport, and Antonio didn't push her to talk. She barely spoke to him on the flight back, either.

How could he even begin to fix this? Tia was going to marry him, which was what he'd wanted since she'd told him the news about the baby: but he could see now that it was only to save her mother from the press. Not because she wanted to be with him.

How ironic that he'd been trying to persuade her to fall for him, and what he'd managed to do instead was let himself fall for her. If he told her how he felt about her—if he could even find the right words—he didn't think she'd believe him. Not now the press were involved.

He'd been honest with her and told her how much he hated palace politics, so why did she believe he'd do something underhand? He really hadn't engineered that kiss. He'd *wanted* to kiss her. Wanted to be with her. He'd been so wrapped up in those unexpected emotions that he hadn't noticed the paparazzi hanging round, and he hadn't seen the flash from the camera.

If only he was good at saying what he really felt. But every time he opened his mouth to tell her, it was as if his throat was filled with sand and the words just wouldn't come out.

When they landed, he said, 'Would you prefer to go to the palace or to go straight back to London?'

'Do I have a choice?'

That really hurt. 'Yes. Of course you have a choice.'

'I want to see my mum,' she said. Before he could offer to go with her, she said, 'And I'll go on my own. I expect you have official duties.'

He needed to speak to his family and the palace secretary, yes, but he wanted to support her. He wanted to be with her; he wanted to make this work. And he rather thought he owed her mother an apology and a personal explanation.

He didn't get the chance to tell her, because she continued, 'And I need to see Giovanni and Vittoria, explain everything to them. They've been so good to me and I feel bad about letting them down. And my friend who was going to share childcare with me. I've let her down, too.'

Guilt flooded through him. She had a whole life without him, and he was ripping her from that support network and expecting her to be in Casavalle with him. She wasn't the only one whose life was changed by this mess. 'Look, I'll sort everything out.'

'That's my life, not yours. *I'll* organise it,' she cut in. Which told him exactly where he stood. She'd see any offer of help as throwing his money around, not a genuine desire to make things better.

'Will you at least let my pilot take you back to London?' he asked.

'Are you worried I might talk to someone in the airport while I'm waiting for my flight and say something I shouldn't?'

He remembered the conversation he'd had with her before, and sighed. 'No, Tia. The media will write what they like.' It hurt that she thought he was so underhand, and he had to draw on every ounce of the training he'd had over the years to remain cool and calm and collected. But he wanted her to know his real motivation, so he said, 'I'm asking if you'll let my pilot take you back because you're six months pregnant and the last thing you need is to wait for hours for connecting flights, perhaps without anywhere to sit if the airport's really busy.'

She turned away so he couldn't see her face, couldn't read her eyes. 'Whatever. I don't care any more.'

And how that hurt, to see her so flat and cold towards him, with all her bubbliness gone. Worse, to know that it was all because of him. That she didn't trust him. 'Let me have a word with the pilot.'

He went into the cockpit and arranged with the crew that they'd take her to London and look after her on the way. 'And can you please make sure that this letter's delivered, and these two parcels go to Tia's mum?'

'Of course, Your Royal Highness.'

'Thank you.' He returned to Tia. Although part of him wanted to take Tia back to the palace before she went to London and at least introduce her to his family, from the set look on her face he didn't think she'd be amenable to the suggestion. 'Please let me know when you're safely back in London.'

She huffed out a breath. 'I'm surprised you don't want to put some kind of tracking device on my phone.'

He winced. 'I'm not trying to trap you, Tia.'

'It feels like it.'

He would've done anything to rewind the last few hours—to go back to the children's Christmas party where he'd felt so happy, where he and Tia had worked as a team and he'd thought they were actually getting closer. And last night, when he'd kissed her under the mistletoe. When she'd fallen asleep on him on the sofa. When she'd shyly asked him to stay with her and he'd woken in the night to feel the baby kicking in her stomach. 'I'm sorry. It's not meant to be…' His throat closed. *A prison.* But hadn't he felt like that at the palace, too? Hemmed in and miserable and trapped by all the politics?

On the other hand, he couldn't just throw Tia to the wolves. The media would make her life miserable without him.

'Safe journey,' he said, and walked to the

door of the plane where the stewardess was waiting.

'Look after her for me, please,' he said.

And his misery must've shown in his eyes, because the stewardess forgot herself enough to pat his arm. 'It'll be all right, Prince Antonio.'

He rather didn't think it would.

And he couldn't bear to look back at Tia and see how much she loathed him.

Antonio strolled off the plane, as cool as a cucumber, and didn't even look back at her. He was clearly so secure in his triumph that he didn't need to make sure his new chattel was sitting exactly where he'd left her.

Tia felt sick.

Right at that moment, she wished she'd never met Antonio Valenti.

There was a volley of kicks, and she rested her hand on her bump. 'I don't regret *you*,' she whispered softly. 'But I thought he was different. That he felt something for me. That he cared. That over the last few days he'd shown her the real man behind the Prince, a man I could really love. But none of it was true. All along it was just to manipulate me into a situ-

248 SOLDIER PRINCE'S SECRET BABY GIFT

ation where I'm forced to do what the palace wants.'

She'd let everyone down. Her mum, the memory of her dad and her brother, her bosses, her friends.

And life was never going to be the same again.

Antonio had everything planned in the official car back to the palace. First, he'd talk to his family; then to the palace secretary, to make sure that their plans for protecting Tia and Grace were completely in place; and then he'd organise Tia and her mother coming to the palace.

Back at the palace, he found his mother in her study, doing something on a computer. He knocked at the door and, when she looked up, bowed deeply, 'Good morning, Mamma.'

She inclined her head. 'Good morning, Antonio.'

'I'm sorry I've...' He took a deep breath. 'I'm sorry I've brought scandal to the family.'

This was her cue to tell him he was a disgrace, how disgusted his father would be, and how she expected better from him.

But to his surprise she stood up, walked over to him and took his hands, squeezing them. 'Welcome home. Where is Tia? Is she resting?'

'No. She's on a plane to London,' he said.

'I see.' Maria looked disappointed. 'I would have liked to meet her, talk with her a little.'

'It's not her fault, Mamma,' he said softly. 'I accept the blame fully.'

'For putting her on the plane?'

He nodded. 'And for the baby—' he choked '—for everything.'

She shocked him even more by touching his face. 'Antonio. A baby is something never to be sorry for. I'm going to be a grandmother. That's wonderful news.'

'Even though…?' He blinked. 'This baby wasn't planned, Mamma. And Tia and I are not married.'

Maria shrugged. 'She seems very sweet, very genuine. You don't know how glad I am that you and Luca have found someone to love, and that Luca's engaged. I know how much Imogen loves him—and, from the look of that photograph, Tia clearly loves you.'

Oh, no, she didn't. She might've started to feel something towards him over the last few days, but he'd managed to kill it. Right now, Antonio was pretty sure that she hated him.

'I've been worried about you,' his mother said. 'I know you took your father's death very hard.'

Antonio closed his eyes for a moment. All the regrets for things that might have been. 'I'll never be able to make him proud of me now.'

'He was always proud of you, Antonio. He just didn't know how to tell you.'

Antonio didn't believe her.

'Your father wasn't an easy man,' Maria said. 'He was a good king, a good man—but he found family life hard. Especially after Sophia walked away from him.'

This was a subject that was never, ever discussed in their family. But Luca had actually mentioned their father's past in public, after he'd got engaged, so maybe things were changing.

'He loved Sophia, but she was from a different world.'

So was Tia.

'She found it hard to deal with our way of life.'

Antonio rather thought that Tia, on the other hand, could deal with anything.

'Walk with me, my child,' Maria said. 'We'll talk in the garden.'

He helped his mother put her coat on—he hadn't had time to take his off—and went with her into the formal garden. Even though it was almost December, there were still a few roses in bloom.

'I love this garden,' she said. 'Your father did, too. He was the one who increased the collection of roses here. He used to enjoy talking to the gardener and looking over rose catalogues with him. I rather think, if he'd had the time, he would have liked to breed his own roses.'

Was she talking about the same man he'd grown up with? Antonio was amazed. 'I didn't think my father—' He stopped abruptly, knowing his words were tactless and not wanting to hurt his mother.

'What?' she asked gently.

He didn't think his father had been interested in anything else other than ruling. 'Being the King was his entire life,' he said eventually.

'It was a very big part, but not all,' his mother

corrected. 'He was a husband and a father as well as the King.'

Antonio struggled to think of a time when his father had showed open affection to his wife or his children. They hadn't even had a pet dog or cat. Even at Picco Innevato, his father had never really switched off. He had been the King first, and everything else had come way down his list of priorities.

As if his mother guessed what he was thinking, she said, 'Vincenzo found it hard to open up about his feelings.'

Yeah. He knew how that felt. He struggled, too.

'And Sophia couldn't cope with royal life.'

'What about you, Mamma?' The question came out before he could stop it. He winced. 'I apologise. That's much too personal. Forget I asked.'

'No, it's a valid question, and you have a point. I should have done more when you were younger,' Maria said with a sigh. 'Your father could never open up because of the way he was raised. In the view of his parents, children should be seen and not heard. They were very closed off and they never told Vincenzo that they valued him for himself—and with hindsight I think he needed to hear that.'

Antonio had never considered it before, and it made him feel guilty. 'I never told him I valued him, either.'

'But he knew you did,' Maria said gently. 'And he valued you, even though he didn't tell you. *I* value you. And maybe I should've told you that more often.'

The lump in Antonio's throat was so huge, he couldn't answer her. But he wrapped his arms round her and hugged her.

Maria stroked his hair. 'Your father was raised to be a king and a statesman, and he made sure he was the very best King and statesman he could be. But he couldn't open up—even to me, sometimes. I think he wanted to try to be closer to you. It's why he suggested that we should buy the house in Picco Innevato.'

'That was my father's idea?' Antonio pulled back, surprised, and looked his mother straight in the eye.

'Yes. So you and Luca would have somewhere to be children, without being in the public eye all the time.'

'That's where I took Tia,' he admitted. 'Picco Innevato.'

'I guessed that,' Maria said gently.

'I asked Miles not to tell anyone anything about where I was going or who I was with.'

She smiled. 'I'm your mother, Antonio. I know things without having to be told. Picco Innevato is where you always go when you need time to think. Where you go to decompress after a bad mission. Luca said that Tia Phillips had been trying to get in touch with you. He assumed that she was someone trying it on and told Miles to ignore her, whereas if either of them had thought to say something to me I could've told them she was Nathan's sister—and I know you blame yourself for Nathan's death.'

Antonio blew out a breath. 'I should've been in that car along with him.'

'I'm very glad you weren't,' Maria said. 'I feel for his poor mother—of course I do, because it's the fear every soldier's mother has, the worry about getting that phone call. I tried never to stand in your way, but I hated you being in danger all the time, and I worried about you every second you were on a mission. So did your father,' she added wryly, 'but he said you needed to do things your own way.'

'He was right,' Antonio admitted. 'I did.'

'I wish he'd written you a letter or something like that, to tell you how he felt. But your father was your father. A different generation.'

'Does Luca know?'

'That your father loved you both and couldn't say it?' She nodded. 'And I think love has changed Luca, too. What happened with Meribel… That was hard for both of them. I feel guilty about that. I should've stepped in and said no, don't agree to marry the girl unless you really love her, because you shouldn't sacrifice yourself for your country.'

'But I thought you said Meribel was crazy to…' Antonio stopped.

'I think,' Maria said gently, 'she will be OK, and in the end she did Luca a favour.'

How would Tia's mother judge him? Would she see him as the man who seduced her daughter, abandoned her, and was now forcing her into a marriage she didn't want? Or would she judge him more kindly?

'So what will you do now, Antonio? About Tia?'

'I...' He sighed. 'I don't know, Mamma.'

'You look as if you're in love in that photograph. And you didn't know it was being taken.'

'She thinks I set it up, to force her to marry me and make the baby my heir,' Antonio said.

'Then you need to talk to her. Find out what she wants. Find out if you can come to some kind of compromise—one where you both win rather than both lose,' Maria advised. 'Tell her how you feel.'

'I don't have the words,' Antonio said.

'Tell her that first. Tell her you find it hard,' Maria said. 'Ask her to help you. And be as honest as you can.'

Once he'd finished talking to his mother, Antonio went to find Luca, who clapped him on the shoulder. 'Congratulations, little brother.'

'Not yet,' Antonio said. 'I haven't quite followed in the footsteps of you and Imogen. I might have messed things up.'

'If you love her,' Luca said softly, 'go after her. Tell her you love her.'

'Is that what you did with Imogen?'

Luca nodded. 'And it was the best thing I ever did.'

Antonio looked at his elder brother. He'd never seen Luca so relaxed and happy. Was it because he was free of the burden of their father's expectations? Or was it love? And, if it was love, could that work out for him and Tia, too?

And how was he going to convince Tia that they had a future?

He still had no idea by the time he went to see Gabriella.

'Antonio. It's good to see you.' She smiled at him 'I saw all the stuff in the press,' she said. 'Are you OK?'

He grimaced. 'I think I might have been an idiot.'

'The girl you kissed under the mistletoe on your front doorstep?'

He nodded. 'I've acted like every other Valenti man—I've expected everyone to fall in with my wishes, and kept my feelings shut away.'

'But you can change that,' she said.

'Yes. It's time things changed in Casavalle,' he agreed.

And then it hit him. He didn't need to shut away his emotions, like he'd always done in the past. Not any more. He loved Tia. Although he knew she didn't love him back, he loved her enough to give her what she wanted. She didn't want to be stuck here in the palace; she wanted to be with her mother in London.

So he'd go to see her. He'd release her from her agreement to marry him, and he'd tell her that he would support her, the baby and her mother however they needed him—just as Tia had always supported her family. If she eventually came to love him, then maybe she would come and live with him. But he was going to put her first.

Before he could arrange a flight to London, Miles called up to see him. 'I was hoping to have a meeting with you and your mother,' he said.

'If it's about Tia, I'm not in a position to discuss anything just now,' Antonio warned.

'It's about Gabriella,' Miles said.

Antonio frowned. 'Surely Gabriella needs to be part of any discussions about her?'

'They're preliminary discussions so we don't need to bother her just yet,' Miles said.

'What about Luca?'

'Prince Luca,' Miles said, 'is otherwise engaged at the moment.'

Antonio sighed. 'I really need to be in London. When do you need the meetings?'

'If your mother is free, we could start now,' Miles suggested.

Maria was available, so Antonio joined her in Miles's office.

'We're having a presentation ball for Gabriella before the coronation, to welcome her to the country,' Maria said.

'That's nice,' Antonio said, wondering just why he was needed at this meeting. Surely they didn't need his input into a ball?

'And we need to think about possible marriages for her,' Miles added.

Oh. So *that* was it. Politics. Antonio folded his arms. 'If you want my honest opinion, I think we should call a halt to this discussion right now. Gabriella should choose her own groom. The last arranged marriage for this family didn't work out well for anyone.'

'That's true,' Maria said, 'and we do need to repair relations between our countries.'

Diplomacy and palace politics. The two things Antonio loathed most. 'I still think Gabriella should choose her own groom. It's the twenty-first century.'

'The word is that Prince Cesar has broken up with his girlfriend,' Miles said. 'And he will be attending Gabriella's presentation ball. He's been called home to welcome her.'

Antonio snorted. 'I hope you're not marking him out as a potential match, Miles. Cesar Asturias is a smooth operator, a playboy who doesn't take women seriously—and I'm not sure he's good enough for my sister.'

Maria said gently, 'Things aren't always what they seem. Remember, the media calls you a playboy as well. Your girlfriends don't exactly last a long time.'

'Because I never found the right one,' Antonio said, 'and I hope that's just about to change.' He looked pleadingly at his mother. 'Do you *really* need me in these discussions? I think you should talk to Gabriella, not to me.' He took a deep breath. Time to tell them how he felt. 'Mamma, Miles—right now, I don't want to be here discussing politics. I want to see Tia. I need to tell her...' The words stuck.

'Tell her what's in your heart,' Maria advised, and gave him a hug. 'Good luck.'

'Good luck, sir,' Miles said, shaking his hand.

To get Tia to really listen to him, Antonio thought, he was going to need more than luck.

And if his words froze on him again when he was talking to her, he was really going to be in trouble. Maybe he should write them down. Just to be sure.

CHAPTER SEVEN

LONDON FELT GREY, dull and dingy after the bright, open spaces of Picco Innevato.

But Tia's time in Casavalle had all been a lie. She knew she'd be very stupid to let herself believe otherwise.

She'd been such a fool. Fancy thinking that Prince Antonio might really care for her.

And now she was going to be trapped into marriage with a man who didn't love her. And was marrying her purely for the baby's sake. This was utterly ridiculous in the twenty-first century, but she supposed things were different when you were a Royal. If she said no, that would mean the press would hound her mother, and Tia couldn't let that happen. She'd do anything to protect her family.

She rested her hand on her bump. 'Why couldn't he have just let us disappear back here?' she whispered.

The baby didn't kick.

Yeah. She had no idea, either.

There was a gentle knock on her door. 'Tia?'

She forced herself to look all smiling and happy. No way was she going to let her mother know what an idiot she'd been. She didn't want Grace to worry. 'Hi, Mum.'

'I thought you might like to see these,' Grace said, coming into the room with a box that Tia recognised as being full of Nathan's things.

'I'm not sure I can face that,' she admitted.

'I think you need to see what's in here,' Grace said gently. 'I'll leave you to it.'

Tia sat staring at the box for a long, long time. Then she removed the lid.

Inside were books and papers. On the very top was a photograph of Nathan and Antonio in their fatigues, smiling, their arms round each other.

Her eyes prickled. How much she missed her brother.

And the man with him in the photograph— that was the man she'd let herself fall for. Except he didn't really exist, did he?

She turned the photograph over and recognised the handwriting on the back. Nathan's handwriting.

A—the dream team on a good day N

Why was a photograph that had a message obviously addressed to Antonio in Nathan's belongings? Had her brother never sent it?

The next thing in the box was a letter. Except it wasn't to Nathan—or from Nathan. It was a letter to her mother.

She was about to fold it up again, rather than pry in her mother's things, when she noticed the address at the top of the page.

Picco Innevato.

Antonio's house.

Why would Antonio be writing to her mother?

Was this her mother's way of trying to tell her something?

Frowning, she read on.

Dear Mrs Phillips

I would like to apologise sincerely to you for the way in which I broke the news of Nathan's death back in January. I should have told you back then that Nathan was like a brother to me, and I miss him terribly. I should also have been there to support you and Tia in your grief.

My only excuse, such as it is, is that I find it very hard to show my feelings. I grew up knowing that duty should always come first. But I want that to be different for my child, whether the baby is a son or a daughter—I know the baby will be loved because Tia is his or her mother, and she's amazing.

I apologise, too, for the way in which I've behaved towards Tia. I truly didn't intend to abandon her, or you. It feels like a weak excuse, but we've had a lot of unexpected events in our family over the last few months and it's been a struggle to deal with them.

Your daughter is an amazing woman. She deserves more than I can ever give her. I have asked her to marry me, and I know she thinks my sole motivation is that the baby will be fourth in line to the throne of Casavalle. But I think a lot of your daughter and I want to be a full part of our baby's life.

I should have asked your permission before asking her to marry me, and I apologise for my forwardness. With your permission, I should like to ask Tia again

*if she will marry me. It has nothing to do
with convention and everything to do with
who she is and how she makes me feel.*

*I am trying to be more open about my
emotions, and I hope that she and our baby
will find it in their hearts to help me.*

*I thought that you might like this pho-
tograph, taken on the mission before Nathan's last one. It means a lot to me, but I
think you should have it.*

With kindest regards

Antonio Valenti

The date was yesterday.

The day of the children's Christmas party.

The day when she'd fallen asleep on the sofa;
when he'd woken her later, she'd realised that
he'd tucked a fleecy blanket round her.

And this letter, where he said that he thought
a lot of her... Antonio wasn't one to talk about
his feelings. He was aloof and formal and *royal*.
So this was tantamount to saying that he loved
her.

She couldn't quite take it in.

Did he love her?

Had she misjudged him?

Frowning, she went out into their kitchen, where her mother was sitting at the table.

'Are you all right, love?' Grace asked.

'Confused,' Tia admitted. 'When did you get that letter?'

'Today, when the car brought you back from the airport,' Grace said. 'And there were two parcels, too, with a note asking me to let you rest for a bit before giving them to you.'

'Parcels?'

Grace indicated the two boxes on the kitchen counter-top, both perfectly wrapped.

Tia opened the smaller one first, and caught her breath. It was the etched glass bauble for the tree.

In silence, she handed it to her mother.

'That's beautiful. Is that where you were?' Grace asked.

Tia nodded. 'He said he bought it for the baby. For the tree.'

'Just like your father and I used to buy a new decoration every year for our tree,' Grace said softly.

With shaking hands, Tia undid the scarlet ribbon on the second box. And she had to bite back the tears when she saw the snow globe nestled among the packing peanuts that protected it: the beautiful filigree star suspended in a perfect orb, except she hadn't wanted to spend the money on herself.

When had he bought this?

Perhaps when she'd been browsing at the candle stall yesterday. He must have gone back and bought it especially for her.

Antonio Valenti might not say a lot, but he noticed things. He'd seen how much she'd liked it. He'd guessed that she didn't want to spend money on herself when she had the baby to think of, and he'd bought it because he'd wanted to do something nice for her, give her something that she'd denied herself.

Especially given what he'd written to her mother, that snow globe was a definite declaration of love. It wasn't the cost of the item; it was the thought behind it.

With horror, Tia realised that he really did love her. And he hadn't been able to tell her exactly how he felt because he'd been brought up in a formal, public world where he'd always felt forced to hide his emotions away. She hadn't made it easy for him to talk to her, either.

This year, he'd been emotionally swamped:

he'd lost his best friend, actually been there when the land mine had exploded and seen Nathan killed; he'd lost his father; and then his life had been turned upside down with the revelations about his brother's fiancée cheating on him and the existence of his half-sister.

And then she'd come along, six months pregnant, and informed him that their one night together had had consequences and he was going to be a father.

No wonder Antonio had had trouble talking about it. It was an overwhelming amount for anyone to deal with, let alone someone who wasn't used to talking about his feelings.

She'd pushed him away because he couldn't tell her how he felt. She'd made the assumption that he'd manipulated the situation with the media, so she'd be forced to marry him and make the baby his heir. Yet had she been fair to make that assumption? If she looked at what he'd actually done... He'd taken her away from the public glare of the palace to his family's private home, the place where he'd spent the summers during his childhood.

He'd tried to make a proper family Christmas for her, choosing a tree and decorations with her and then cooking her Christmas dinner. He'd agreed to fill in for the Father Christmas who'd broken his leg—the kind of role she knew he'd never done before, simply because she'd asked him to. He'd kissed her under the mistletoe, shown her with actions rather than words how he really felt about her.

And, because he hadn't had the words to tell her, she'd assumed the worst.

How could she have been so stupid—and so unfair?

And this was the last straw. For the last year, she'd tried so hard to be strong, kept all her worries locked inside. Now tears slid down her face. She cried not just for her brother, but for the man she loved, for her mum, for her dad, for her baby and for herself.

Grace wrapped her arms round Tia. 'It's going to be all right, love.'

'How can it be? I've messed everything up. I've hurt Antonio; and I just don't know what to do.'

'I do,' Grace said. 'Talk to him. Go back to Casavalle and tell Antonio how you really feel about him.'

'I can't leave you in London, Mum.'

'Yes, you can. I'll be fine,' Grace said firmly. 'I'm managing. Yes, I'm still going to have bad days, but I have support here. And I've always felt terrible about you putting your own life on hold because of me. I know you love me and you worry about me—but that's how I feel about you, too. And it's about time you started living your own life instead of trying to fit everything around me.'

'But, Mum—'

'But nothing,' Grace cut in. 'All I want is to see you happy. Go to Antonio and tell him how you feel about him.'

'What if he's changed his mind? What he said in that letter... I didn't give him a chance to tell me any of that.'

'Give him a chance now. It's not too late.'

'But...how can he be with me? How will his family ever accept me?'

'They'll love you as much as he does,' Grace said. 'I know your father's family didn't accept me, but not everyone is like them.'

'But he's a prince, Mum!'

'Think about how he was with you in Picco Innevato,' Grace counselled. 'That's the private man—the man he really is. One who cares.

One who might not be very good at telling you how he feels, but look at that photograph.' She brought the newspaper over to Tia, showing her the front page. 'The look on his face when his hand's on your bump and he's feeling the baby kick. You're looking at him with exactly the same expression. You love each other, Tia. You just need to give him the chance to learn how to tell you.'

Tia hugged her mum and cried even more, letting out all the misery and loneliness she'd hidden away for the last year.

And then, once she'd washed her face, she started packing.

She was halfway through when their doorbell rang.

'I'll get it,' Grace called.

When her mother didn't call her, Tia continued packing, assuming that it was a courier wanting them to take in a parcel for their neighbour.

But then Grace knocked gently on her door. 'I'm just going next door to see Becky. And you have a visitor.'

'A visitor?'

'Remember what I said,' Grace said softly. 'Give him a chance.'

Tia's pulse leaped.

Had Antonio come for her?

'I've made you both a cup of tea. You need to talk,' Grace said.

Tia followed her mother into the kitchen. Antonio was sitting there as if he belonged—but how could a prince belong to her world?

'Good luck,' Grace said, patting his shoulder, then left the flat.

Oh, help.

What did she do now? What should she say?

In the end, she fell back on a simple, 'How was your flight?'

'Fine, thank you.'

His face was as impassive as ever. She didn't have a clue what was going on in his head. Was he here to follow up on the letter he'd written to her mother, to try to tell her how he felt? Or was he here because he'd had time to think about it and had changed his mind?

'Why are you here?' The words slipped out before she could stop them.

'I've come to release you from your agreement to marry me.'

It shocked her so much that she ended up sitting down at the table with him, knowing that her knees simply weren't going to support her.

He wasn't here to follow up on that letter. She was too late. He'd changed his mind.

'What I did was selfish,' Antonio said. 'I railroaded you into agreeing to marry me. I didn't give you the choice and I was wrong. You're a strong, independent woman and you're amazing.'

Tia couldn't quite get her head round this. Was he breaking up with her, or was he trying to tell her something else?

'I'm not very good at showing my emotions,' he said. 'That's true of all the Valenti men— my father, my brother and me. But when you stayed with me at Picco Innevato, you taught me so much. You taught me how to feel—and that it was OK to admit I love someone.'

She stared at him, still not quite comprehending.

'I'm making a mess of this,' he said with a sigh. 'I'm trying to tell you that I…' He paused.

That he what?

That he loved her?

He pulled a piece of paper out of his pocket

and looked at it. '"I love you, Tia. I want to marry you, but only if you want to marry me. I'm not asking you out of a sense of duty or of honour, just because you happen to be pregnant with my baby. I'm asking you because I want to be with you."'

She looked at him. 'Are you *reading* that to me?'

'Yes,' he said. 'Because I can't do the words otherwise. They freeze in my throat. I don't know how to say it. That's why I wrote everything down on the plane, in case I froze. So, yes, I'm reading from a script, because otherwise I can't do it and I don't want you to think...' He blew out a breath. 'I'm off script. I'm stuck.'

He loved her.

So much that he'd written it down to make sure, with his usual military precision, he got it right.

'Go back on script,' she said softly. Because she needed to hear what he had to say.

His face brightened, and he looked at the paper again. '"I know you're strong enough to cope with just about anything on your own, and I admire your strength, but you don't *have* to be on your own. If you'll let me, I'll be right by your side, supporting you all the way. You might have to yell at me from time to time, and remind me to tell you what's in my head instead of assuming that you already know by some weird kind of osmosis, but I'll be there with you all the way. I'll be the best husband I can possibly be to you, and the most loving dad I can possibly be to our baby—and, if we're lucky, to our future babies.'" He lifted his chin and put the paper down. 'I'm going to do it without the script now. I love you.'

'You love me.' She still couldn't quite take that in he was actually saying it to her.

'If I'm really honest with you, I fell in love with you before I'd even met you,' Antonio said. 'The way Nathan described you, so full of courage and strength, I knew you were the kind of woman I wanted to be with. But when I finally met you everything had just gone horribly wrong. I felt guilty that Nathan died.'

'It wasn't your fault.'

'I still felt guilty,' Antonio said. 'Survivor guilt, maybe, but guilty all the same. Plus you were his little sister. You were off limits. I was all mixed up, wanting you and feeling guilty about that, too. I'd wanted to tell you and your mum how much Nathan was loved, how much everyone thought of him—and instead I just closed off and made a mess of it.' He grimaced. 'When I saw you again at the charity gala, I felt so bad that I hadn't stayed in touch.'

'Don't be so hard on yourself. Your father died, and you were needed at the palace,' she said gently. 'I understand.'

He took her hands. 'I still should've done more, and I'm sorry I let you down.'

'It's OK. You're here now—and you're not the only one who shut your emotions away,' she told him. 'I couldn't cry for Nathan because I thought I had to be strong for Mum, and I was wrong, too.'

'You've been crying now.' He lifted one hand to stroke her face.

She nodded. 'For everything. For you, for Nathan, for both our dads, for my mum, for the baby...'

Antonio leaned over the table and kissed her lightly. 'You don't have to be strong all the time—just as I don't have to be strong and silent, either. We'll have each other's backs. And

278 SOLDIER PRINCE'S SECRET BABY GIFT

we can be ourselves with each other and with our baby.'

'I love you, too.' She swallowed hard. 'And I knew before you told me that you love me, because you bought me the snow globe. You noticed I liked it and guessed that I didn't want to spend the money on myself. It's the thought that counts more than the gift.'

'True. You've taught me that, too.' He looked at her. 'So, what now?'

'I told you about my mum—how my dad's family didn't like her.'

'And you worry that my family will feel that way about you?'

'I don't have a drop of blue blood in my veins. How am I going to fit in?'

'By being yourself,' he said. 'Just so you know, my mother told me to come and see you and tell you how I really felt. She said those photographs on the news made her feel better, made her feel that I'd found someone to love and who loved me all the way back. And she's thrilled about becoming a grandmother.'

'Really?'

'Really,' he confirmed. 'Luca told me to go after you and tell you how I feel about you. So did Gabriella. You'll be more than welcome in Casavalle, and so will your mother. I want to… I want to be a family with you, Tia. You come as a package, and that's fine by me—because I come as a package, too.'

Then, to her surprise, he slid off his chair and got down on one knee. 'I know I'm rushing you and you don't have to answer me now, but will you marry me? I'm not asking you because I think it's my duty or yours, but because I hope we both feel the same way about each other,' he clarified. 'Because we both love each other, and we want to make a family together.'

She knew that speech had been tough for him. Telling her how he really felt. Particularly as he'd done it without working out the words and writing them down first.

But it was how she felt about him, too.

'Because we both love each other, and we want to make a family together,' she repeated. 'Yes.'

He got to his feet in what looked like a nanosecond, and wrapped his arms round her. 'I love you, Tia. It feels weird saying it, but I'm hoping the more I tell you, the easier it'll be, and that you'll come to believe me.'

'I believe you now,' she said. 'I love you, too.'

He kissed her lingeringly, and there was a volley of kicks in her stomach.

He broke the kiss. 'Is that baby-speak for "Get a room"?' he asked wryly.

'No. I think it's baby-speak for "I approve",' she said with a smile.

'Good. Let's go and tell your mother the news. And then I'd like to take you, your mother and the baby home with me to Casavalle. Home to our future.'

'Our future,' she echoed.

EPILOGUE

Valentine's Day

TIA PEERED OVER the edge of the cot at the sleeping week-old baby. 'I can't believe we made someone so perfect,' she whispered.

'Nathan Vincenzo Valenti. The most beautiful baby in the world.' Antonio slid his arm round her shoulders. 'It doesn't get better than this, does it?'

'I didn't think I'd ever be this happy,' Tia said. 'But your family's wonderful and they've all made me feel so welcome—Mum, too.'

'Because you're part of us,' Antonio said simply. 'You have been, since the first moment you walked into the palace and gave my mother a hug. And definitely since you stood in our private chapel and said your wedding vows. You've got the Valenti name now. No escape for you.'

She twisted round and kissed him. 'I don't want to escape. I love you, Antonio.'

'Good. Because I love you, too.'

They were still gazing besottedly at their sleeping son when Grace walked into the room.

'Is he asleep?' she whispered.

'Yes,' Antonio said.

'Then I'll come back for a cuddle later,' Grace said.

They followed her out into the living room. 'Are you having lunch with us today, Mum?' Tia asked.

'It's lovely of you to ask, but I'm afraid I can't—I'm already going out,' Grace said.

'Anywhere nice?' Tia asked.

Grace blushed. 'Miles says it's a mystery tour.'

Tia exchanged a glance with Antonio. They'd both noticed that the palace secretary was spending a lot of time in Grace's company. Miles and Grace seemed to have bonded over organising Tia and Antonio's wedding in a private ceremony in the middle of December, and that blush just now made Tia pretty sure that her mother was going out on a date rather than simply doing a bit of sight-seeing.

'Have a wonderful time, Mum,' she said, hugging her mother. 'And don't overdo it.'

Grace smiled. 'I know better than to do that, love. Besides, Miles won't let me. I'll see you both later and I'll be back to cuddle my grandson.'

Antonio smiled at Tia as his mother-in-law left their apartment. 'I have a feeling there might be a little bit of romance in the air.'

'Me, too, and I'm glad,' Tia said. 'Mum's been on her own for much too long. And I like Miles. He's a nice guy. Kind.' She smiled back at him. 'Even if he did refuse to let me talk to you for weeks.'

'He was doing his job. Being diligent. And he'll look after Grace the same way,' Antonio said. 'And now it's my turn to look after you. Sit on that sofa and put your feet up, because a cheese toastie and a cup of tea are in your very near future.'

She grinned. 'Are you ordering me about, Your Royal Highness?'

'I can try,' Antonio said, laughing. 'But no.

We're a team. And I only made that suggestion because I know it's your favourite. You can have anything you like.' He kissed her lightly. 'If anything, I'm yours to command.'

She scoffed. 'I'm no general.'

'No. You're just gorgeous,' he said. 'I love you, Tia. I never thought I'd ever be this happy in Casavalle. But things have changed in the palace. Everywhere feels lighter and happier and less formal. You, Imogen, Gabi and Grace have kind of taken over the palace, and my mother's just blossomed, having daughters and a new best friend. And with you and our baby here with me... My world's complete.'

'Mine, too. I love you,' Tia said, kissing him. 'We don't have to have lunch, you know. We could just go and snuggle up under the covers.'

'That,' Antonio said, 'is an excellent idea.' He scooped her up and carried her into their bedroom.

But just as he was about to deposit Tia on the bed, they heard a wail.

'We,' he said, 'are going to have to wait. Because it sounds as if someone's hungry.' He settled Tia back against the pillows. 'I'll go and get him. And then I'll make you that cup of tea.'

'And join us, I hope,' Tia said. 'Because there's nothing more perfect than snuggling up with my gorgeous son and even more gorgeous husband.'

Antonio kissed her again. 'I agree. You're the wisest of women, Tia Valenti.'

Tia made herself comfortable, ready to feed the baby. The newest Valenti Prince had stolen everyone's heart, and he'd made a huge difference to life at the palace. Their baby was an unexpected gift who'd brought Antonio's family closer together, cracking the reserve and formality at the palace to let the warmth of love radiate through.

Love and tenderness that weren't kept just for private moments: Antonio was openly affectionate, holding her hand and sliding his arm round her and stealing kisses. He'd lost his cold, remote shell for good, and the real Antonio was definitely the man of her dreams.

'Penny for them?' he asked, walking in while rocking the baby on his shoulder.

'Just thinking how lucky I am,' she said.

'How lucky we are,' he corrected. 'And this is something I'll never take for granted. A happiness I always want to share with the world. Because love is the best gift of all.'

* * * * *

LET'S TALK

Romance

For exclusive extracts, competitions
and special offers, find us online:

- ▣ facebook.com/millsandboon
- ◙ @millsandboonuk
- 🐦 @millsandboon

Or get in touch on 0844 844 1351*

For all the latest titles coming soon,
visit millsandboon.co.uk/nextmonth

*Calls cost 7p per minute plus your phone company's price per
minute access charge

Want even more
ROMANCE?

Join our bookclub today!

'Mills & Boon books, the perfect way to escape for an hour or so.'

Miss W. Dyer

'Excellent service, promptly delivered and very good subscription choices.'

Miss A. Pearson

'You get fantastic special offers and the chance to get books before they hit the shops'

Mrs V. Hall

**Visit millsandbook.co.uk/Bookclub
and save on brand new books.**

MILLS & BOON